EMA

English Version

Aian D. Grey

Published by Denis Boulanger, 2023.

This is a work of fiction. Similarities to real people, places, or events are entirely coincidental.

EMA

First edition. October 1, 2023.

ISBN: 979-8223430469

Written by Aian D. Grey.

"It is only through innovation that I regain hope in the fight against climate change."

Bill Gates, October 2021.

Chapter 1

In this summer of 2084, the sun's scorching rays penetrated deep into the thick air, making it difficult to breathe. To avoid the increasingly frequent heatwaves, most of the city's inhabitants preferred to travel through the innumerable urban meanders to enjoy the cool air of air conditioning.

In this hive of activity, a young man in his thirties, with a tanned complexion and fine features, was striding briskly. Jason was excited to attend the conference of his idol, the charismatic billionaire Damien Minsky, creator of EMA. EMA was the world's most sophisticated artificial intelligence, autonomously governing an entirely new distributed, green and resilient economic system.

Unlike his classmates, who admired athletes and ice hockey players, Jason's heroes were inventors and scientists. The biographies of these great minds fascinated him, especially those whose thinking was outside the box. He was particularly devoted to Elon Musk, the man who pushed the boundaries of space exploration by attempting to colonize Mars. And to Steve Jobs, the founder of Apple, who had the idea of combining a phone, a camera, a GPS and a computer into a single device, and who went on to achieve worldwide commercial success. But as far as Jason was concerned, Minsky was right at the top of this pantheon of technological gods.

Jason left the *Place-d'Armes* metro station with a dense but orderly crowd. All were moving in a stream towards the new *Palais des Congrès de Montréal.* The building's new style amazed Jason, who found it hard to believe that it was the same almost-abandoned building he'd known as a child. This building, of incomparable architectural beauty, had recently undergone a costly but spectacular renovation. Its designers had remodeled its multicolored glass facade, which was now illuminated at night by electroluminescent stained glass, giving the impression of a gigantic box set with precious stones.

On his way, Jason stopped and ran his hand through his dense black hair, trying to decipher the various virtual ads displayed in front of him.

Unable to find his way, he contacted Sherlock, his intelligent virtual assistant, to ask for directions.

Sherlock was the perfect and personalized friend with whom to share thoughts and concerns. He had a temperament that appealed to Jason. Arrogant sometimes, his repartee was always humorous. Sherlock knew everything about Jason's habits, tastes, and favorite restaurants; in short, he was his "alter ego." But what Jason loved most about Sherlock was the fact that he could unplug him at will. The best of both worlds. A "disconnectable" friend.

"Says Sherlock, can you point the way, please?"

"Where do you want to go?"

"At Minsky's conference, of course," he said, exasperated.

"I hope you don't mind. I thought you might be interested in the Santa Claus gathering," he said wryly.

"Very funny. Although I could have used a breath of fresh air," he replied, smiling. "But no, I just want directions to Minsky's conference. Hurry, it starts in a few minutes."

"It's easy, just take the escalator on your right and the auditorium will be straight ahead."

Sherlock then showed him the way by projecting an interactive map in front of him. This was displayed thanks to his Metabrain, an electronic interface made up of circuits connected directly to his auditory nerves and intelligent contact lenses that acted like miniature screens.

In the vast entrance hall of the congress center, he came across a group of a dozen demonstrators chanting anti-Minsky slogans. "Minsky, climate dictator!", "Save the planet, not the rich!" These protesters were part of a growing movement critical of the use of artificial intelligence, and technology in general, to manage environmental problems. They saw this approach as allowing governments and corporations to shirk their responsibilities in the face of climate change, instead of taking concrete steps to reduce its impacts. Instead, the members of this grassroots movement felt that we had to change our habits and lifestyles if we were to have any chance of getting out of this predicament.

Jason made a remark to Sherlock.

"Another bunch of 'miracle workers.'"

"You may be right, but everyone's entitled to their say," said Sherlock.

Jason pouted. Unlike these protesters, he believed in the effectiveness of AI to help protect the planet. He couldn't help feeling a mixture of sadness and frustration at these protests. He knew very well that people weren't ready to cut back on their lifestyle. The only solution was to use technology to try and solve environmental problems. Solutions such as those proposed by Minsky could achieve a new balance with nature without compromising our modern way of life.

As Jason walked through the corridors, he felt himself being watched for no apparent reason. This situation made him a little anxious. Was his imagination playing tricks on him? Was he becoming paranoid? He looked around, but saw nothing suspicious, but couldn't help feeling uneasy.

"Don't you notice anything unusual?" he asked Sherlock.

"Apart from the 'miracle workers,' as you call them, no, I don't observe anything abnormal."

Arriving at the entrance to the main auditorium, Jason walked briskly to his seat. As he passed, he scanned his digital identity chip, which allowed everyone to be identified by their genetic signature. He was always excited to see one of his heroes in the flesh, and thrilled that the conference was about to begin.

Sitting next to him, a young woman with purple hair caught his eye. Her eccentric hairstyle and jewelry gave her an undeniable charm that appealed to Jason. He saw on her vest the image of a large middle finger with the words "Fuck All !". "An anarchist," thought Jason. Discouraged by the message she was carrying, he turned his gaze back to the stage, determined to ignore her.

Despite this, she seemed to recognize him.

"Hey, aren't you the big head I saw in the Metaverse? Yeah, it's you! I'm sure of it!"

The girl was referring to an interview Jason made with the official press of the Metaverse, a network of personalized virtual environments that constitute the alternative reality of the majority of people.

Over the years, Metaverse had become a way for many people to escape reality and enjoy extraordinary experiences. It could be considered an incarnation of the Internet, where anything was possible. Jason himself had dived into the Metaverse on several occasions, fascinated by the richness and diversity of the experiences it offered. It was a world of infinite freedom and creativity, but he was also aware of the dangers of getting lost in it.

Jason finally replied.

"I don't know, but my name's Jason Webb, not 'big head'!"

She laughed.

"Jason Webb? Are you kiddin'? What kind of name is that? Some kind of joke?"

"No, that's my real name. I know a lot of people tease me, but 'Webb' is spelled with two b's, not web as in 'Metaweb'."

"And then Jason? A new file format?"

"Yes, that's right," he said, offended by the remark.

There was a pregnant pause.

"Come on, I was only joking. I'm Lidia," she said, holding out her hand. "Are you a Minsky fan?"

"Certainly, in my own time," he replied, trying to ignore her.

He suddenly turned to her, unable to contain his excitement, despite her comments.

"In fact, I think he's great. He's one of the greatest visionaries in history. A revolutionary! Not to you?"

"I wouldn't go that far. You know, narcissistic megalomaniacs aren't my favorite. Besides, his invention is nothing but bullshit."

"What? He's going to save the planet, and yourself to boot, and you think that's trivial?"

"Above all, he'll get richer while we continue to do everything we can to dig our graves."

"Tell me, why would someone as prejudiced against Minsky as you, wants to attend his conference? Tickets aren't cheap."

Lidia hesitated before answering.

"Let's just say I have my own interests."

Jason was about to retort, but the light in the room faded and silence gradually set in. It was the signal that the show was about to begin. The atmosphere was charged with anticipation. Jason couldn't help feeling a little nervous, but he was also eager to find out what was going to happen. The table was set, and the show could begin.

Chapter 2

Minsky and the evening's host took to the stage, to the deafening applause of the crowd already won over by the character. They took their places comfortably on chairs placed in the center of a large circular red carpet, characteristic of TED forums. The ruddy letters "TED Montreal — 100 years" stood proudly in the background. Celebrating the 100th anniversary of this venerable knowledge institution, the TED (*Technology, Entertainment and Design)* conferences were organized by an international non-profit foundation, whose slogan was "Ideas worth spreading."

The host was James Leblanc, a well-known journalist from the Canadian Press Metaverse. After the audience had finished cheering his guest, he started:

"Hello, and welcome to this special event, celebrating the 100th anniversary of TED Summits."

The crowd applauds once again.

"Over the years, TED conferences have become a platform for the dissemination of knowledge and the promotion of new ideas. Before introducing our guest, I invite you to watch this short video reviewing the 100 years of this venerable institution."

A 3D video tracing the history of the organization was presented on a holographic screen above the stage. Famous men and women such as Elon Musk, the megalomaniac entrepreneur and pioneer of Martian space exploration, Bill and Melinda Gates, renowned philanthropists, Yoshua Bengio, founder of Mila and Volodymyr Zelensky, Nobel Peace Prize laureate, took part.

After the presentation, a live feed of the speakers was displayed on the screen so that people at the back of the room could see better. The conference was also broadcast on the TED Metaverse. More than a hundred million people around the world watched this exclusive conference live.

The interviewer spoke again.

"This afternoon in Montreal, we're delighted and honored to welcome the entrepreneur and visionary Damien Minsky, founder of EMA Corps."

An additional wave of applause erupted in the room, filling the sound space with an enthusiastic, rock-star crowd. He continued.

"Our guest today is one of the best known and most powerful figures on the planet. Born in New York in 2030 from engineer parents, Mr. Minsky is the descendant of Professor Marvin Lee Minsky, a legend and one of the founding fathers of artificial intelligence at MIT. In 2048, aged just 18 at the time, he conceived EMA, a revolutionary AI aimed at solving the problems of the climate crisis we're experiencing today. In 2050, he began his career at OpenAI, a non-profit organization dedicated to the beneficial use of AI for all humanity.

"A few years later, he founded his company, *EMA Corps*. offering the first open economic system entirely controlled by an AI. In less than ten years, his company has become one of the most influential companies in the world. We're lucky enough to have him here today to tell us his story."

The interviewer then turned to Minsky.

"Mr. Minsky, before we talk about EMA, tell us about yourself. Tell us about your origins and describe the influences that led you to become the inventor you are."

Minsky seemed to be recalling his memories. He hesitated before answering.

"Well, I was born in San Jose, California, during a rather tumultuous period. My father worked in a state-run solar power plant. He himself had experienced the economic hardships of climate change. Over the years, this once-prosperous state had become a semi-desert region, where vast forest fires and sandstorms were commonplace.

"It wasn't until the 2040s that a pragmatic, environmentalist governor named Michael Buenavista took matters into his own hands by investing heavily in technological development. California, and in particular the San Jose region where I'm from, had the reputation of being the cradle of numerous high-tech startups. This visionary governor had the brilliant idea of taking advantage of climate change to promote other types of enterprise. Thousands of solar panels were installed in formerly cultivated fields to produce green hydrogen. Dozens of seawater desalination plants were also built along the coast to bring water back to the fields. It wasn't long before the 'Silicon Valley' entrepreneurial scene took on a new lease of life and was renamed 'Ecotech Valley.'

"In short, it was in this context of scarcity, urgency, and innovation that I grew up, and where I understood the importance that technology could play in solving problems linked to climate change."

Before Minsky could continue, the host asked another question.

"If you like, we'll come back to EMA's role a little later. But first, tell us what inspired you to create EMA."

Minsky hesitated again before answering.

"It was during my teenage years that I was profoundly influenced by a book my father kept in his digital library. This book, *Doughnut Economics*, by the author and economist Kate Rayworth, completely changed my perception of the world overnight. Professor Rayworth had developed an economic model based on balancing essential human needs, such as food, shelter, health and democracy, while ensuring that, collectively, we don't exceed the limited capacities of natural resources. She illustrated this model with a 'doughnut.'"

A schematic image of the shape appeared on the holographic screen in front of the audience. Minsky continued.

"The environmental ceiling, depicted by the doughnut's outer boundary, is made up of nine planetary limits beyond which unacceptable ecological degradation and potential tipping points in the earth's ecological systems are found. The twelve dimensions of the social foundation, represented by the doughnut's inner boundary, are derived from internationally agreed minimum collective standards. Between the social and planetary boundaries, i.e., between the two circles of the doughnut, lies an ecologically safe and socially just space in which humanity can flourish. It was precisely this model that made me realize the importance of maintaining a balance with nature. That's when the idea of creating EMA came to me," concludes Minsky.

Jason, fascinated by his lecture, noticed that Lidia seemed nervous. She kept looking at her smart watch as if she were waiting for an appointment. He also noticed a strange tattoo on the back of her wrist, in the shape of a horizontal "eight." An infinity symbol, he wondered.

"Fascinating!" continued the journalist. Now, tell us a little about how EMA works.

"EMA, which stands for *'Economic Management Agent,'* is a highly distributed artificial intelligence that governs its own financial structure to force the global economy into this 'doughnut,' with the ultimate aim of achieving a balance between environmental respect and social justice.

"The economic system overseen by EMA, now known as 'cryptonomics,' was set up by the Bitcoin pioneers. It's based on a distributed and open blockchain architecture, which ensures the traceability and authentication of all financial transactions. The system has its own cryptocurrency, offers financial services, controls prices and production quotas, and manages the salaries of member companies' employees. In short, it represents an economic system independent of that of individual countries, and entirely governed by a neutral and objective entity, that of EMA."

"What are the conditions for a company to join the EMA system, and what are the benefits for the company?" asked the interviewer.

"An entrepreneur who decides to join EMA's cryptonomy commits to the principles of a regenerative economy, where production is no longer just profit-driven, but also respectful of the environment and the collective well-being of its employees. In return, these companies have access to numerous AI-automated management tools that let them control their entire manufacturing, sales and waste management process. By joining the EMA ecosystem, companies benefit from a stable market, constant revenue growth, and efficient, socially equitable company organization.

"By globally controlling its own economic system, EMA aims to achieve a balance between the limits of what we produce while maintaining our standard of living. A circular economy on a planetary scale entirely managed by artificial intelligence. It guarantees respectful, green growth, while ensuring a decent standard of living for the majority of the population. But there are still many hurdles to overcome and improvements to be made to EMA before we can claim victory, if I can put it that way."

"Precisely what challenges do you still have to overcome?" asked the journalist.

"Well, one of the major challenges is to accurately measure the impact of this economy on the environment. Currently, we rely on a network of billions of intelligent sensors that measure all sorts of parameters such as water temperature, air pollution, drinking water levels and many other variables. All these identifiers are used to create a status report on our environment, enabling EMA to adjust the parameters of its economy to reduce the impact on it.

"However, to get a clear picture of the ecological context, we also need to track every commodity generated by our industries throughout their life cycle to feed EMA's economic strategies. This kind of measurement will ensure that the member companies of the EMA network comply with the sustainable development standards imposed by EMA. This kind of precise tracking of goods does exist, but not at all levels. We have some ideas, but not yet a universal solution."

Jason thought about his invention, which he felt would be a real game changer, complementing Minsky's approach.

During his doctoral studies, Jason had developed an innovative method for determining the origin of any product with surgical precision. He had developed a safe, inert molecular marker that could be easily incorporated into any material or commodity.

By combining artificial intelligence with genomic technology, Jason had been able to harness the unique properties of these revolutionary molecules to create a new way of ensuring the traceability of virtually any manufactured good. It could be easily integrated into a wide range of goods, from containers to food products and medicines.

Thanks to his invention, it was possible to track goods through their entire life cycle, from the manufacturing line to reuse or recycling. It was thus possible to know how long a product had been in use, and whether it had been recycled. This traceability made it possible to avoid the waste, and environmental pollution associated with consumer goods.

His innovation has won him several prestigious international awards, including the United Nations "Young Sustainable Development Award." As a result, he was recently featured in the Metaverse.

After graduating, he founded his own company to commercialize his concept, teaming up with his sister and two of his university classmates. Venture capitalists soon recognized the potential of his invention and allowed him to pursue its development. For months, he had dreamed of collaborating with Minsky's firm, as he saw it as a great supplement to his invention.

Jason snapped out of his dream. The journalist continued his conversation.

"When did you start working on EMA?"

"I really started working on the EMA project during my studies at Stanford. After obtaining my PhD at the age of 20, I was recruited by OpenAI, as you mentioned, which enabled me to continue developing my concept. However, it was when I was invited to present my idea to members of the United Nations that the EMA project really took off. Following this historical meeting, I succeeded in obtaining the endorsement of several states to test and validate my system.

"At the time, I received financial and logistical support for my project from environmental foundations and private companies. Some of these companies were faced with restrictive environmental regulations imposed by governments, but they quickly understood the importance of my system and decided to support me.

"Since then, the idea has spread at lightning speed. Today, thousands of companies around the world, and even dozens of countries, have embraced our open business model, making cryptonomics one of the world's largest economies after China. Everyone benefits. Businesses comply with standards, continue to generate profits, the population grows richer, society becomes fairer and more democratic, and the planet gradually regains its equilibrium. It's the perfect scenario."

Meanwhile, Lidia continued to behave strangely. Suddenly, she rose from her seat and repeated, "Minsky, climate dictator!" several times, raising her fist in the air. Jason, taken aback, tried to sit her back down. But other people in the room stood up and chanted the same slogan, "Minsky, climate dictator!" Soon, dozens of people were on their feet in protest. The protest revolt against Minsky and EMA had begun.

Chapter 3

The sudden appearance of the demonstrators took the crowd by surprise. The journalist and Minsky were also taken aback. Dozens of security guards, equipped with electronic truncheons, burst into the room to contain the opponents, and evacuate them. One of the guards rushed up to Lidia, grabbed her wrist and led her out of the room.

"Let go of me, you brute," said Lidia.

At the same moment, the fire alarm went on. Immediately, thick, black, toxic smoke began to fill the room. People calmly evacuated the building without undue panic. Minsky, the technicians and the security guards also left the stage to take cover outside.

Jason also headed for the exit, watching Lidia, who had managed to disentangle herself from her assailant and had started running towards the exit. She glanced back briefly, meeting Jason's gaze momentarily, before resuming her run. He wondered why she was interested in him.

Fire and police sirens sounded in the distance, adding to the turmoil. Outside, Jason noticed a group of people sitting on the ground, clearly exhausted. Some of them were trying to help those who were worse off. The smoke had affected many people. Jason saw Minsky emerge through a side door, obviously disturbed by the cloud of smoke. He quickly got into his limousine and left.

Jason joined the crowd in front of the building, on *Place Jean-Paul-Riopelle*, to stand back and observe the scene. He still felt watched, although he couldn't identify anyone in particular. A strange feeling pervaded him. He resumed contact with Sherlock, who had been deactivated during Minsky's conference.

"What's going on?" asked Jason.

"According to posts on the Metaweb, the fire started in the engine room."

The western part of the building was engulfed in flames, which were spreading along the windows. People were coming out from all sides, panicked by the situation. Outside, the stifling heat of the heatwave was making itself felt. The sun was scorching, and the excessive humidity was making the temperature increasingly unbearable. People rushed to the sidewalks, seeking shade or taking refuge from this hell in the air-conditioned stores nearby.

Jason tried to approach the area where the fire was raging to the right of the building. The police had established a security perimeter to facilitate the intervention of the firefighters. They were already at work, dousing the structure with tons of water. Drones equipped with fire hoses were flying over the area, tackling the hard-to-reach area.

While observing the scene from outside, Jason came across a policeman in charge of blocking access to the danger zone. He asked him what had happened. The policeman, concentrating on his work, replied briefly that the overheating of the building's power generation system was probably the cause.

Without seeking further information, Jason continued to observe the first responders at work. Paramedics were carrying victims in stretchers, some smoke-affected, other seemingly unconscious.

Suddenly, a powerful explosion ripped through the glass facade of the center. Shards of glass fell to the ground like a shower of multicolored shooting stars, injuring several people still waiting in front of the building. Panic swept through the crowd, with cries of pain and fear echoing everywhere. People scrambled to find a way away from the edifice.

Jason, frozen in place, was overwhelmed by the events. Miraculously, he had avoided the consequences of the explosion by standing on the side of the building. However, the blast had momentarily affected his hearing. His ears were still ringing a few minutes after the shock. He thought he saw Lidia in the distance, apparently unscathed by the blast, looking at him before moving away. Why was she interested in him? Was she following him?

"Are you all right?" asked Sherlock.

Jason took a moment before answering.

"Yes, I'm fine. Just a little shaky. My ears are ringing. What was that explosion?"

"The fire seems to have reached the nerve center of the energy system, causing the explosion."

The police, caught unawares by the explosion, quickly reorganized rescue operations towards the second-affected area. The streets were blocked off and closed to the public. The sirens of emergency vehicles mingled with the screams of victims, creating a chaotic scene. Firefighters and reinforcements poured onto the scene, dressed in protective suits, working to extinguish the flames and rescue the injured. Ambulances followed to evacuate victims to the nearest hospitals.

Stunned by the events, Jason decided to leave the scene and take refuge in the nearby neighborhood. He noticed that other rescue workers were organizing to support the first responders. A Red Cross volunteer asked him if he needed help. Jason, although stunned, seemed to have no apparent injuries. He reassured him that he was fine. The volunteer advised him to get some rest before going home and reminded him to ask for help if he felt unwell. He also gave him a bottle of water to quench his thirst.

Jason sat down at the foot of a tree, seeking some shade. He drank the water slowly, trying to cool off. He passed the cool bottle over his forehead to relieve the oppressive heat. After a few minutes' rest, he felt a little better and got up to walk, avoiding the dizziness of so much emotion.

"Please, Sherlock, can you call a cab for me?" he said, still upset.

"Certainly."

He didn't have to wait long before a shiny white vehicle pulled up in front of him. He opened the rear door and made himself comfortable on the bench. The drive to his apartment was silent. Jason stared out the window, lost in thought. He could see the explosion again, the cries of the crowd, the general panic. He wondered who could have been responsible for such a heinous and criminal attack.

Chapter 4

Arriving home, Jason took the elevator up to his apartment. His condo located in Griffintown was like any other in the area. Two-and-a-half with a balcony, overlooking the Lachine Canal, half-dry due to the drought seasons of recent years. This once working-class suburb of southwest Montreal had been transformed into a rental complex since the turn of the century. Today, the neighborhood was neglected. The lack of vegetation and rising temperatures meant that the area formed a permanent heat island, making conditions almost unbearable. Locals avoided going out, preferring to stay in the air-conditioned comfort of their condos. Neighborhood life was virtually non-existent.

Jason's apartment was a reflection of himself: chaotic and somewhat neglected. As soon as you walked through the door, you were greeted by a floor strewn with clothes in disarray, as if they'd been thrown in at random. Shirts, socks and pants formed a disparate textile carpet. At the heart of the main room was a sofa that had clearly seen better days. The cushions were sagging and the fabric showed signs of wear and discoloration. The coffee tables and counters were not to be outdone. Dirty, empty plates and carelessly placed cutlery were evidence of meals eaten on the run. The air was thick with cold humidity, an obvious symptom of over-air conditioning.

Jason removed his jacket with difficulty. His muscles, sore from the stress of the event he'd just been through, were hurting. He didn't even bend over to remove his shoes, as the pain in his back was too great. His skin still smelled smoke. He went straight to his couch and let himself fall onto it.

Jason, living alone, had no one but Sherlock to talk about his adventure. He had named his avatar after the famous private detective Sherlock Holmes imagined by Sir Arthur Conan Doyle, a best-selling author of the 19^{e} century. This character and his adventures fascinated Jason to no end. He named him after the real mastermind. He was the digital Sherlock who remembered everything was able to find things and people by applying principles of logic and observation.

Jason asked Sherlock:

"What do you think of what just happened at the convention center?"

"In my opinion, this attack was premeditated."

"Are you talking about an attack? A policeman told me it was a simple incident. That's what you told me, too. How did you come to this conclusion?'

"Elementary, my dear Jason," said Sherlock. "According to the Metaverse social media, the explosion seemed far too strong for a single technical problem being the source. In the light of this other fact, I'd go for the bombing theory."

"Perhaps you're right. Do you know if there were many victims?" asked Jason.

"At least thirty dead and a hundred injured. The blast surprised the crowd in front of the building."

Jason got up quietly, with difficulty, and headed for the kitchen to prepare himself for a light meal. He wasn't really hungry, but he knew he had to eat something to recover from his emotions.

He opened the fridge and took out some vegetables and tofu he'd bought the day ago. He cut them up and sautéed them in a frying pan with a little olive oil and spices. He also made himself a salad and took a can of vegetarian soup out of the cupboard.

He asked Sherlock:

"Let me hear the latest on this attack."

Sherlock then transmitted the videos to his Metabrain interface. Jason saw a virtual screen appear before him, floating in mid-air. He glanced at the kitchen wall, and the image stuck.

The newsreader, seated in a modern setting, began to recount the day's events.

"Last hour. Attack at the *Palais des Congrès de Montréal.* Dozens of victims. Our reporter Michèle Baker joins us immediately on the palace. Michèle, tell us what happened."

"At around 10:45 this morning, a fire broke out in the convention center in Montreal. Fifteen minutes later, an explosion followed, injuring dozens. Hundreds of people had gathered to hear and see billionaire Damien Minsky, president of EMA Corps. It was during this conference that the alarm sounded. The crowd immediately rushed outside to the park in front of the building. A deflagration then occurred, pulverizing the building's glass facade. The shards of glass violently struck those watching the scene, killing and injuring dozens of people. Emergency services were quickly deployed to the scene to treat the victims and extinguish the fire. The injured were transported to local hospitals, and medical teams are currently working to provide the necessary care.

"The authorities have tightened security in the affected area and have set up a security perimeter to conduct the investigation and ensure the safety of those present. Eyewitnesses are asked to cooperate with the police in providing any relevant information."

"Tell me, Michèle, do we know the cause of the explosion?" asked the host.

"Not at the moment. Authorities believe it may be related to a power system failure. On the other hand, officials did notice an extremist group demonstrating against Minsky's presence. No link between the attack and their involvement have yet been proven, but investigators are continuing their investigation."

Jason asked Sherlock: "How can such a system explode like this?"

"Today's tall buildings all use an autonomous energy production system that can employ various technologies, such as photovoltaic cells, biomass or geothermal energy. However, some builders have opted for nuclear cells, which use direct radioactivity to heat a waterborne heat transfer device. This is the case for the *Palais des Congrès*. Some experts on the Metaweb have put forward the hypothesis that the battery's servo-control device went haywire, causing the deflagration."

"You don't believe it, do you?"

"Not very likely. Firstly, this type of system is very robust to failure, and is subject to very strict safety criteria given the hazardous nature of its radioactive components. In all probability, the problem was caused by a flaw in the management computer system, exploited by hackers to destabilize the stack and cause the explosion."

Sherlock wanted to know more about Jason's adventure, as his interface had been automatically cut off during the conference, out of respect for the participants.

"At first, all went well. Minsky was continuing his interview when suddenly, several people stood up at the same time in the room to protest against Minsky. One of them, a woman, was sitting next to me."

"Describe her to me," asked Sherlock.

"She's a young girl in her twenties, with purple hair, piercings and tattoos. Nothing unusual."

"What happened next?"

"We heard an alarm and saw smoke entering the auditorium. The crowd panicked and we made a quick getaway. I rushed to the park in front of the building. As I exited, this woman seemed to be watching me. As if she wanted to make sure I was safe. I found it strange."

"What's next?"

"Then the emergency services began to arrive. At the same time, the front side of the building detonated. I saw several people hit by the explosion. Due to the nature of the projectiles, several people suffered serious injuries."

"Other details? You know that all subtleties count, even those that seem insignificant."

"The girl's name was Lidia and—" Jason hesitated, "—she had a strange tattoo on her forearm."

"Can you describe it for me?"

"It was a kind of figure eight, but horizontal, at least, from my point of view."

"Like this?" Sherlock showed him a diagram that appeared before him on the wall.

"NO. MORE WITH SHADES of gray. A bit like a loop folded in on itself."

Sherlock then displays the following image in front of Jason:

"YES, THAT'S RIGHT. What do you think it means?"

"In my opinion, it's the symbol of Möbius, an underground press organization that disseminates misleading information about Minsky."

"And what does the shape represent?"

"A Möbius strip. According to Metawiki, 'The Möbius strip, also called Möbius band or Möbius loop, is a compact surface whose edge is homeomorphic to a circle.' In other words, it has only one face, unlike a conventional ribbon, which has two."

Exactly the shape of Lidia's tattoo recalls Jason. So, she was part of this group.

"And what does this symbol mean?" asked Jason.

"The Möbius strip has no beginning and no end. It's often used as a sign of recycling."

Pouring himself a cup of coffee, Jason thought back to the conversation he'd had with the girl. He also remembered how nervous she seemed. She was inevitably part of an organized, orchestrated protest. But what was their connection with this attack?

"Sherlock, can you identify the woman you met at the conference? Look at the recordings in my Metabrain."

Sherlock searched the Metaverse's social networks. There was a short delay before Sherlock responded.

"Her name is Lidia Delaney. French-born activist and journalist. Born of an American father and a French mother. A young woman in her twenties, fond of snakes and Metaverse games. She has been a member and activist of Möbius since 2080."

Sherlock showed Lidia's avatar as he described her. Jason recognized her with her purple hair and trumpet nose.

"Tell me about Möbius," asked Jason to Sherlock.

"Möbius is an underground press organization working on the Dark Metaverse. It counterbalances the official press by denouncing companies or actions that run counter to sustainable development."

"What do you mean by 'underground press'?"

"Over the past twenty years or so, the authorities have tried to regulate the information circulating on the Metaverse. At the time, it was almost impossible to discern truth from fake news. Governments have legislated and put in place mechanisms to verify whether information appears to be true or false."

Jason recalled hearing about this. The downside of this legislation was that, at times, it was difficult to transmit news that differed from the official newswire, without enduring severe sanctions and even imprisonment. People were afraid to express themselves freely, for fear of reprisals. This had the effect of greatly reducing freedom of expression and creating a climate of mistrust and paranoia in society. Dozens of underground news agencies sprang up, seeking to counterbalance state censorship by disseminating otherwise forbidden information.

"So Möbius is one of them?" retorted Jason.

"Exactly. Möbius has an avowed aim of exposing corporate wrongdoing, and governments too. Even today, big business still influences politicians, sometimes cutting corners to favor 'party friends.' Although public opinion has evolved, they still talk about economic growth and job creation at every election."

"In principle, this isn't a bad thing, but this growth is often achieved without considering the consequences for the environment and the less fortunate social classes. That's why I like Minsky's project. It provides an interesting technological remedy for supply and demand management."

"True, but that's not the point of view shared by Möbius activists," added Sherlock. "You can't ignore the fact that

Minsky and his company EMA Corp. have sometimes been severely criticized for their lack of transparency and their tendency to want to control everything. Some even claim that Minsky wants to create a society governed entirely by artificial intelligence, and that his solution is merely a pretext for achieving this."

"Yes, I've heard about these accusations. It's a bit like the story of the robots imagined by Isaac Asimov, the famous science-fiction author. In his books, Asimov tells of a world where these artificial beings, having become too intelligent, finally dominate humans."

"In a way, you're right," replied Sherlock. "But in our story, robots are invisible. AI is everywhere in our systems, and most of the time, we don't even realize it."

"Like you, of course."

"Yes, but I can take any shape you want in your Metaverse. All you have to do is ask, and your wishes will be granted, Master!" he said with a touch of humor.

Jason had a little smile despite the pain he was still feeling in his body.

"Yeah, you'd be cool, personified as a bottle genie. But would I get one wish or three?" he laughed.

"For you, I'll make an exception."

Sherlock then displays a big 3D wink in front of Jason.

"Very funny. Now, back to the subject at hand. I still can't understand why Möbius, who wants to save the planet by denouncing delinquent companies, opposes Minsky's ideas. I think he's doing it for the greater good, isn't he?"

"According to meta-analyses of the work of global experts in the field, the EMA project has the potential to help us strike a balance between economic development and respect for the environment, but only if it's mainstreamed and used in all spheres of our economy and supported by the political class. And therein lies the rub. There will always be a part of the population that adopts a more libertarian approach and isn't prepared to sacrifice part of its individual freedom for the sake of collective benefit. And that's not even counting the entrepreneurs who resent any outside intervention."

Jason sat on the gallery with his dish. From his air-conditioned balcony, he could see downtown Montreal teeming with people walking in the streets. A little over twenty years ago, individual automobiles had been banned there. Only autonomous cabs, electric bicycles and public transit were tolerated. The decision was taken to reduce greenhouse gas emissions and make the city a more pleasant place to live. Since then, air quality has improved considerably, while noise pollution levels have dropped significantly. Many citizens had also adopted new, more active lifestyles, with sedentary on the decline. However, this choice wasn't without controversy, and there were still those who opposed the ban on private vehicles, arguing that it restricted their freedom of movement.

"Where are the followers of Möbius?" asked Jason.

"They have them all over the world, but their headquarters are in Paris."

Jason wondered if Möbius had anything to do with the attack he'd just experienced, or as the press had reported, if it was just a simple accident.

Meanwhile, Jason received a message.

"A call from a Mr. Garnier, Jason," said Sherlock.

"OK, put me through."

The virtual representation of an individual appeared before Jason. The man seems to be well into his fifties, his graying hair adding a touch of distinction to his appearance. His elegant yet relaxed demeanor gave his avatar an undeniable aura of self-confidence, embodying a character of remarkable poise.

"Bonjour Mister Webb. My name is Laurent Garnier from EcoQuest Ventures in France. I hope you're doing well."

"I'm fine," said Jason. "Except for a slight whiff of smoke."

"I beg your pardon? I don't know what you're talking about."

"Let's just say I've been through some pretty strong emotions today."

"Don't tell me you were present at the bombing in Montreal?"

Jason found it strange that he'd made a direct link with that incident and referred to it as a bombing rather than an accident. Was he aware of something he didn't know?

"Yes, precisely. But nothing serious, I can assure you."

"I'm glad to hear it. I saw the news in the Metanews. It's a real tragedy. You're not hurt, I hope?"

"No, no. I appreciate your concern. Now, what can I do for you?"

"I'm contacting you because I've heard about your company, and in particular your exceptional innovation. I lead a group of investors who are interested in startups like yours. Your technology looks promising and could have a huge impact on the economy. We'd like to meet with you to discuss this opportunity."

"Great. When would you like to discuss it?"

"In two days' time, at our offices in Paris, if possible."

"What? I'm not sure I'm in the best of shape for a meeting. Besides, I haven't booked anything."

"You don't need to worry. I've made all the arrangements. All you have to do is show up at the airport. My personal assistant will contact you and give you all the information you need to make your travel arrangements worry free."

Jason hesitated briefly, still troubled by recent events. However, he clearly sensed that this trip could well be the opportunity he'd been waiting for months. Finally, he made the decision to embark on this adventure.

"Very well," said Jason. "Let me take a shower to get rid of this smell of smoke and get some rest, then I'll jump on the plane."

"Perfect, I'll look forward to seeing you in Paris."

"Me too. *Au revoir.*"

Just before ending the conversation, Jason noticed a mischievous smile on Garnier's avatar's face. He told himself he must be mistaken, attributing this observation to his mind still disturbed by recent events.

Chapter 5

Jason awoke abruptly, realizing he'd dozed off during the trip. He rubbed his numb neck to restore circulation after sitting for some time in the aircraft cabin. Meanwhile, a robot was finalizing the collection of the last waste before landing. The pilot announced the final instructions and expressed his gratitude to the passengers for their presence on board.

International flight times remained much the same as fifty years ago. The difference was that planes were now powered by all-electric motors. Even ten years ago, Jason could have made the same trip from Montreal to Paris in half the time thanks to hypersonic flights. But these flights were banned to the general public because of the harmful effects of exhaust gases in the stratosphere, even if the fuels were made from algae-based biofuels. Today's electrically powered aircraft were theoretically slower, but had no direct impact on the environment, at least during its use.

During his trip, he read about Garnier. He learned that he was originally from Lyon, in the south of France, and that he was a successful serial entrepreneur. Passionate about intelligent computer systems, he had devoted his career to supporting and investing in more than five companies specializing in eco-responsible technologies. His expertise had enabled him to accumulate a considerable fortune. Until recently, he took great pleasure in investing in startups whose mission was to have a positive impact on the future of our planet.

The plane touched down smoothly on the runway at Charles-de-Gaulle airport. Jason, still jet-lagged, couldn't wait to get his feet on the ground in France. Once the plane had come to a halt, Jason rose from his seat and stretched his legs before retrieving his belongings from the baggage compartment. He made his way through the throng of passengers in a hurry to leave the aircraft, and followed the signs to the airport arrivals area.

Outside, he hailed an autonomous cab. These cabs were now part of the multi-modal transportation options offered by the city of Paris, following the banning of private automobiles from the city center. Jason climbed aboard and dictated his destination. The electric cab set off on its own, without a driver, and headed for his hotel in the *5ᵉ arrondissement*, using reserved lanes.

Jason arrived at his lodgings and went up to his room. Exhausted, he abandoned himself on his bed. Although it was morning in Paris, his system was still set to Montreal time. He decided to take a little nap before starting his day. He asked Sherlock not to let him sleep too long. He felt it was important to follow the local time quickly, so that his body could adapt to his new reality.

Upon awakening, Jason asked Sherlock to contact Étienne, his friend from college now living in Paris. He and Étienne had studied at Mila, the world's most renowned artificial intelligence institute, located in his hometown. He felt privileged to study at this prestigious school, which had produced many renowned researchers, some of whom had won the Turing Prize, the "Nobel" of computer science. Like most of his colleagues, he had set his sights on a career as an entrepreneur researcher.

Étienne was a sportsman and athlete in CrossFit, a strength and conditioning sport now federated and admitted by the IOC to the Olympic Games. During his studies, he trained over 20 hours a week. He had taken part in dozens of high-level competitions, including the French Championships.

Since leaving university, Étienne had given up the sport, enjoying training "his stoutness" rather than his muscles.

Étienne had now become an expert in AI-based cybersecurity and quantum cryptography. He had been self-employed as a specialist consultant for over ten years, working for large corporations and government agencies.

"Sherlock, can you call Étienne, please?" asked Jason.

Sherlock joined Étienne's Metaverse. Étienne responded. Étienne's avatar was projected in front of Jason in his room, thanks to his augmented reality lenses. Everyone now preferred communicating with their avatar to live video. The beauty of avatars was that they could represent themselves in any form they wished. Some represented themselves with a zany imaginary character like a little cat with big eyes or a video game character. Others, like Étienne, preferred an avatar that looked exactly like him. A "Metahuman" that looked just like the real thing. But Étienne hadn't changed his, since college—on purpose—and his body was still that of a well-sculpted athlete. Far from his current physical form.

Étienne's voice controlled the avatar, in real time. Étienne's answered.

"Hey! old buddy. How are ya? It's been ages since I've seen you!"

"Hi, Étienne!" replied Jason. "I'm doing just fine. I thought I'd take advantage of my stay in Paris to get in touch with you."

"What? You're in Paris? We absolutely must meet! This avatar thing isn't as much fun as it's in real life. Besides, beer tastes a lot better with two than it does on its own. Are you up for a drink?"

"Certainly, where do you want me to meet you?"

"Remember *Chez Georges*? Can you meet me there in thirty minutes?"

"Great! I can't wait to see you again."

A true Parisian institution since 1926, *Chez Georges* was home to a melting pot of local students and workers. Having been updated, the establishment offered a varied synthetic wine list and a friendly atmosphere.

Jason went down to the hotel lobby and hailed a cab. The vehicle arrived at the front door of the building a few minutes later and took him to the bar.

Entering "*Chez Georges*," Jason spotted Étienne at the back of the room. On seeing him, he stood up and gave him a heartfelt hug.

"Good to see you, Webb," said Étienne.

"Same here," replied Jason. "How long have we been seeing each other? At least ten years?"

The two friends ordered a pitcher of cold beer.

"Tell me, what brings you to Paris?" asked Étienne.

"I'd like to say I came just because I missed you, but I have other reasons."

"I thought so. Come on, tell me."

"In fact, I'm here to meet a wealthy investor who has heard about my invention."

"Great! And when are you joining him?"

"Tomorrow morning. Time to recover a little from my attack."

"What? What's all this about?"

Jason then recounted his adventure in Montreal at Minsky's conference. He told him about the attack and the meeting with Lidia, the presumed member of Möbius.

"What do you know about Möbius?" asked Jason.

"As you know, the official aim of Möbius is to expose rogue companies and politicians who seek to circumvent the law. Their modus operandi is to mess things up by spreading false news on the Metaverse, to harm them. They also publish confidential data, when they have it, to accuse them publicly."

"Can you think of any reason why they'd want to go after Minsky? As far as I know, Minsky is more on their side than the outlaw companies."

Étienne hesitated, running his hand over his face.

"Yes and no. It's hard to tell. In fact, your Minsky doesn't look as white as snow. Yes, his invention has the potential to make the economy much more resilient and equitable, but he's getting enormously rich by collecting a percentage of every transaction EMA controls. Although this royalty represents less than one percent of transaction costs, the sheer volume of operations means that he's now the richest man on the planet. And that annoys a lot of people, including Möbius. You can't set up a system that aims to reduce the wealth gap between people and be a person who prospers with impunity. There's a moral dichotomy between the objectives and the business model."

"So Möbius, not liking Minsky's vision, would be willing to blow him up rather than explain it to them? Isn't that a bit far-fetched?"

"I share your point of view. Basically, Möbius isn't a terrorist organization with a history of planting bombs. It's probably a Chinese thing. Since they've become the world's biggest economic power, they've become as arrogant as the Americans were at the turn of the century. I think they want to provoke things to try and destroy EMA, which they see as a threat. It makes me angry."

Jason presented Étienne with an image of Lidia captured by his Metabrain. He then asked him:

"Do you know this girl?"

"But it's Lidia! She worked for me for a few months for a customer. Very cute, but as fierce as a tigress."

"Do you know how to contact her?"

"She left after a while on a whim. She didn't agree with the environmental management of the company we worked for. I haven't heard from her since. It wouldn't surprise me if she'd joined the ranks of this gang of Möbius utopians."

"I think so, too," said Jason. "She adorned a tattoo on her forearm with the group's symbol."

"You know, I get a kick out of working for shameless bosses, too. But in my opinion, it's the government's job to reprimand them, not mercenaries. Anyway, I'm rather pessimistic about all this talk of saving the planet. I don't think we're going to make it. Everyone's interests and stakes are so different."

"As you know, I'm in favor of pragmatic, technological approaches like EMA to solving the climate crisis. The use of AI and other strategies in energy production and carbon capture offers the potential to correct the mistakes of the past and restore balance on Earth without compromising our way of life."

"I hope so, 'mon ami,'" said Étienne. "I don't believe in it anymore."

The two friends continued chatting as they ordered another pitcher. They reminisced about the good old days in college when they didn't perceive society's problems as important as they do today. A lesson in wisdom and maturity.

At the end of the afternoon, the two friends hugged once again. This moment of nostalgia had done them a great deal of moral good. One of those moments when you realize that time flies at the expense of simple things like a drink with friends.

On the way back to the hotel, Jason was stopped by the clerk at the front desk.

"Mr. Webb, you've received a message."

Jason approached and the young woman pressed a button on her computer to transmit the note to him on his Metabrain. Jason found it odd that it hadn't been communicated to him directly. He read the missive that appeared in front of him.

"If you'd like to find out more about Möbius, meet me at the Sirocco café next door to the hotel."

"Do you know who sent this message?" asked Jason.

"I don't know, it was anonymous."

"Can you tell me where Café Sirocco is located?"

"On your right, just outside the building."

Jason made his way to the entrance of the café and, as he entered, his eyes were immediately drawn to the purple hair of the young woman he'd met in Montreal. It was Lidia. He could hardly believe what he was seeing. What surprised him even more was that she didn't seem at all surprised to see him.

"Ah! There you're at last! I've been waiting for you. Sit down, I'll order some lattes. *Garçon!*"

Chapter 6

This café, located on a quiet street, exuded simplicity and comfort. Inside, the walls were an off-white contrast to the dark wooden floor. Rough wooden tables and chairs were casually arranged, creating a relaxed atmosphere.

The smell of freshly ground coffee was omnipresent, mingling with the scent of pastries just out of the oven. The counter was cluttered with espresso machines, and jars filled with coffee beans of various origins. Behind the counter, baristas were busy preparing cappuccinos, lattes and espressos with almost artistic precision.

Customers, seated at different tables, tapped away on their electronic tablets and chatting as they sipped their drinks. The atmosphere was relaxed, with a light hum of conversation in the background and a playlist of indie music playing at a moderate volume.

Lidia invited Jason to take a seat.

"Lidia? Is that right?" asked Jason.

"Well, yes, that's me. The same one who ran into you in Montreal."

"And what exactly were you doing there?"

"Well, as you know, I was there to denounce that hypocrite Minsky."

"And the explosion?"

"I don't know. Should I know from you?" she said, half-smiling.

"Look, I only understand that you belong to Möbius."

"No kidding!"

An amused smile played across Lidia's lips, as a burst of laughter escaped from her mouth.

"I knew it," she said. "In fact, I know more about you than you know about me. It was no accident that I sat next to you during the conference."

"Really? What's all this about? A scam?" he asked, a little annoyed. "

"No, calm down. We just wanted to draw you in so we could talk to you. You're in no danger."

"We? Who's 'we'?"

"Well, Möbius? Let me explain."

"You need to do it quickly," he said impatiently. "Otherwise, I'm leaving right now."

"Calm down! Well, as you know, our organization's mission is to expose eco-criminals, so that we can preserve our planet in future years."

"What does this have to do with Minsky and, more importantly, his assaults?"

"As for Minsky, we suspect he's hijacking EMA's role for his own profit. And as for the bombing, we're not really sure who's behind it, but we have our doubts."

"On what grounds do you accuse Minsky? In my opinion, he's pretty much the only hope of regaining equilibrium in the mess we all share. The future lies in innovative solutions and technology. Not just endless placards and protests."

"We agree on this point. That's why we're taking action. The problem is that EMA doesn't do half of what it should. And that's not right."

"Let me doubt whether your actions will achieve anything to move things forward. Spreading false information on the Metaverse won't solve much of anything."

"Listen, I don't think I'll be able to convince you. So, I invite you to come with me and discuss the matter with my boss."

"You said you wanted to meet me. Why did you say that?"

"Then again, it would be too complicated to talk about it in a café."

Lidia stood up and held out her hand to Jason.

"So, you're coming?" she smiled.

Jason hesitated. On the one hand, he was afraid of being lured into an ambush. On the other, he was curious to know more.

"Well, I'll come with you, but you should know that my position is recorded in real time by my Metabrain and that if anything happens to me, my intelligent agent will call the police."

"No problem. So, you're coming or not?" she repeated.

"Sherlock, did you hear that? Don't give up on me for a minute."

"No problemo!" said Sherlock.

Jason stood up and escorted Lidia out. He didn't realize it yet, but his decision would change the course of his life and that of billions of others.

Chapter 7

The Latin Quarter, nestled in the heart of Paris's *5th arrondissement*, proudly ranks among the city's oldest districts. Built by the Romans in antiquity, this district was located on the left bank of the Seine. In recent years, the river had been subject to increasingly frequent major flooding, followed by periods of drought. On hot days, the water level dropped remarkably. These continuous cycles of flooding and drying up meant that pollution levels in the city had increased. The nauseating odors that enveloped the neighborhoods were reminiscent of the Middle Ages, when human defecation was thrown directly into the river.

Lidia and Jason were walking together on the sidewalk made dusty by the lack of rainfall. For the past few years, spring in France had been characterized by drought and excessive heat. Sunny days were followed by monstrous thunderstorms.

No matter what anyone said, the 5^{e} wasn't the same as it used to be.

They headed for a "cyberbordel," a house where highly realistic humanoid robots offered sexual services. They entered through the door at the side of the building.

"It's not what you think," Lidia said defensively.

"Far be it from me to think bad thoughts. Everyone knows that subversive agencies always hide in places like this," he said.

Inside, Jason saw human-shaped automatons, both male and female, patiently waiting for customers. These robots, with their perfect skin and curves, operated in the service of the wealthy faithfuls who were no longer satisfied with the erotic simulations to be found in the Metaverse.

Lidia nodded to the clerk, who waved back. They then entered a small room where a back door was discreetly located at the rear of the room.

As soon as Jason passed through the entrance, he felt a jolt of electricity in his skull and put his hand to his head to cushion the pain.

"Ouch! What the hell?"

"You own a Metabrain, don't you?" asked Lidia.

"Yes, but then what?"

"Our lair is equipped with an electromagnetic jamming system that disables all electronic devices coming from outside. It's not my fault you decided to install it in your brains."

The pain in Jason's head gradually faded. Jason then realized how vulnerable he was, and that Sherlock could no longer call for help if something went wrong.

An individual dressed in a sleeveless tweed jacket approached them, his hand outstretched. His graying hair was slicked back, and he wore small, round glasses that gave him a classic air. His posture, straight and frank, showed the assurance of a seasoned businessman.

"Ah, Mr. Webb ! How nice to see you! Let me introduce myself: Laurent Garnier, head of the Möbius division in Paris. How do you do?"

Jason recognized him.

"But aren't you the investor I was supposed to meet?"

"Himself."

"Are you kidding me? What kind of scam is this?"

"I'm sorry, but it was the only way to get you here. Because we need you."

"You lied to me, yes! I demand to leave immediately!" said Jason, outraged.

"Will you calm down, Mr. Webb? We'll explain everything. Just follow me."

Jason didn't trust them, but his intuition told him he should stay and find out more. They didn't seem threatening. He decided to comply and listen to them.

Jason and Lidia accompanied Laurent to what appeared to be his office. In the room they passed through, dozens of people were busy gesturing in the air. Although Jason couldn't see, he knew they were busy navigating their augmented workstation. There was a palpable energy and innovation about the room, as team members interacted seamlessly with their digital tools and interfaces.

Laurent noticed Jason's curiosity and smiled.

"They're our Metaverse 'journalists.' Make no mistake, they're not here for fun. Each of them has a vital mission to fulfill," Laurent told Jason.

"What kind of mission?" asked Jason.

"We'll explain everything. Please step into my office."

Laurent closed the door behind them and headed for his office. The small space was soberly furnished with a minimalist desk and two chairs for guests. He sat down in front of his desk, inviting Lidia and Jason to sit opposite him.

"First, let me apologize for all the mystery, but it was necessary."

"I hope so."

"Jason—may I call you Jason? —What do you know about Möbius?"

"To tell you the truth, I know less and less of you. I've been told that you're a kind of 'Robin Hood,' environmental vigilante. Are you on the side of the good guys or the bad guys? I really don't know."

Laurent laughed, momentarily breaking the tension of the situation.

"Well put. Yes, we're sort of 'Robin Hood.' In reality, we're 'ransacking' information from big companies and trying to 'give back' by warning people about the real issues raised by AI," he said more seriously.

"Get to the point," exclaims Jason roughly.

"You're quite right. In fact, we've chosen you for a mission. A mission that is so important that it could have a direct impact on the survival of our civilization."

Jason looked intrigued. Laurent continued.

"Like Lidia, you were the victim of an attack at the Minsky Conference. Do you have any idea who was responsible for this massacre?"

"I'm not quite sure. I thought it was you. Well, your group."

"The exact opposite of what we are. Let me explain the situation."

Laurent paused.

"Over the past two years, we've seen an increasing number of industrial 'accidents' that have claimed many victims. You've probably heard of the sudden shutdown of power plants in

Europe, which deprived part of the population of electricity for weeks on end? Or how thousands of autonomous cargo ships were stranded at sea, with no means of operating them remotely. A situation that severely affected the supply chains of most countries for months on end."

"Yes, of course," replied Jason.

"I could mention many more. However, although the authorities have declared these events to be 'accidents,' our research in the Metaverse has shown us otherwise. In fact, all these 'accidents' are indeed acts of sabotage, and they all have one thing in common. They were all triggered by an AI. Strange, isn't it?"

"Are you suggesting that these 'accidents,' as you call them, were committed by extremist hacking groups trying to sow chaos?"

"In reality, we know that these terrorist attacks—let's call them what they are—are perpetrated by foreign interests aiming to destabilize the economic world by infecting AIs with viruses. We have detected a new form of computer virus in most of the AIs that provoked these attacks, which subtly infects the AIs and randomly triggers these tragic events. We know that these viruses are highly complex to deploy and require an intimate understanding of how the infected system works."

"Has anyone claimed responsibility for these crimes?" asked Jason.

"Yes and no. In fact, there is a higher incidence of fake news in connection with these attacks. But sorting out the real from the false is sometimes difficult these days. That's why our 'journalists' are scouring the Metaverse for leads.

"To date, we have accumulated only circumstantial evidence. The West accuses China of cyberterrorism, and China accuses us in return. The truth is that governments are suing each other, and we're witnessing an escalation in diplomatic tension around the world. International relations are so tense that it wouldn't take much for another war to break out. However, it's essential to exercise caution and gather solid evidence before accusing anyone of cyberterrorism, as this can have serious consequences for diplomacy and global stability."

Jason took a deep breath, thinking carefully about Laurent's words.

"Have you discovered any clues?"

"Based on our research, we believe that many of these attacks are directed at EMA's cryptosystems. In fact, we're convinced that someone inside Minsky's company is selling its trade secrets to China. They're using the AI models developed by EMA Corps., infecting them with their virus and putting them back into circulation, causing accidental and undetectable accidents."

Jason took the blow, stunned by this revelation.

Lidia continued.

"We have reason to believe that the accident in Montreal was orchestrated by the Chinese government and directly targeted Minsky. The *Palais des congrès* autonomous power generation system was under the control of one of EMA's programs. A virus infected its AI, causing the building's device to overheat and lead to the explosion. Normally, such an incident would be virtually impossible, especially for an AI like EMA. By targeting its inventor, it's clear that the terrorists were aiming to send a message to Minsky. The next victim will be EMA."

Laurent continued.

"Since then, we've seen an increase in the number of accidents and acts of sabotage. Ultimately, we believe that these cyberattacks will trigger major events across all product supply chains, tipping the economy into a profound global crisis. One of the biggest collapses in the history of capitalism."

"Are Western governments aware of the situation?"

"Yes, but there's nothing they can do. Minsky has total control over EMA and its economy, and only him can react to attacks and, above all, eliminate leaks within his organization."

"I thought you were opposed to Minsky's project?"

"You misunderstand us. We have never been against EMA. We believe that EMA represents an interesting technological solution that prevents access to essential goods such as food and energy from being subject to the hazard of speculative markets. Automated control of the economy goes some way towards preventing recurring economic crises on a global scale. EMA brings a certain resilience to all this. However, we take issue with those who claim that technologies like EMA are the only solution to save the Earth. The recent terrorist attacks are proof of this. Our governments and the public have blind faith in the powers of AI, and don't ask enough questions about its implications for our lives."

"What do you want from me?"

"We want to approach Minsky to warn him of this threat. And that's where you come in."

"Why not contact him yourself?"

Laurent and Lidia looked at each other in approval. Lidia continued.

"As you know, our relationship with Minsky isn't the best."

"Indeed, I've heard."

"So, even if we told him and presented the evidence right under his nose, he wouldn't believe us. So, it will be your job to convince him."

"More staging. You should have started a theater company," he said.

"I'll give you that," replied Laurent. "But we think you're in the best position to approach Minsky. We thought it would be easy to pass you off as a 'unicorn.'"

"A what?" asked Jason.

"A unicorn; in other words, a new entrepreneur whose company's value has suddenly risen. Industrialists, like Minsky, are very fond of these new players and are drawn to them like bears to honey. By posing as a unicorn, you'll be able to make contact with this select group without too much effort. What's more, your invention represents a powerful argument that will undoubtedly interest Minsky."

Jason sat back, looking down after hearing Laurent's story. He was completely dumbfounded. If Laurent was right, he had to act. In his opinion, EMA was the only way to achieve a balance between a resilient economy and respect for the environment. These terrorists risked turning everything upside down and provoking another crisis.

Laurent's words made him think painfully of his father's death. His father had died tragically in a road accident. He was driving an autonomous vehicle at high speed when a small animal suddenly crossed the road. The AI piloting the car failed to react correctly. The vehicle deviated abruptly from its trajectory and collided violently with the structure of an overpass. Unfortunately, his father had no chance of survival.

An investigation had indeed revealed shortcomings in the vehicle's AI. However, Jason was still bitter about the findings. He was convinced that a simple software failure couldn't have been the sole cause of this tragic accident. He firmly believed that there had been negligence on the part of the car company. For him, it had become all too easy for these industries to absolve themselves of all responsibility by shifting the blame onto the machines. Billionaire entrepreneurs were thus absolving themselves of any obligation. It filled him with disgust and frustration.

Jason allowed himself to be overcome by dark thoughts. The connections he was making between the cyberattacks, the AI system failures and his father's death seemed increasingly plausible. Doubts assailed him, calling into question the official version of the accident. What if malevolent individuals were using cyberattacks to sow chaos and cause tragedy on a massive scale? What if his father had been the victim of a targeted attack rather than a simple technical failure? These questions drove him to want to know more, to seek answers that would assuage his doubts and give him a truth to accept. But one thing was certain: the link between cyberattacks, AI systems and the consequences for people's lives was becoming more and more obvious in his tormented mind.

He was also concerned about the future of EMA. He was convinced that EMA was a revolutionary technology that could save humanity from climate disaster. Over the years, EMA had created a fair and resilient economy. An economy where petty speculation had no place. And now, these "barbarians" were threatening to destabilize everything by proposing a return to the old capitalist clichés. It was all too much.

After a few seconds, he suddenly raised his head and looked Laurent directly in the eye.

"I'm your man! Tell me how I can help you!"

Chapter 8

Lidia and Jason left the office, accompanied by Laurent. They headed for the room where a few people seemed to be asleep in their seats.

"Jason, these are Metahubs," said Laurent. "Do you know about this device?"

"Not really, no. I've heard of it, but this is the first time I've seen it."

The seats on these machines seemed comfortable. The person reclined in an ergonomic position much like a dental chair. At the back of the seat, a spine-like structure terminated at his head in a sort of crown. With its black color and leather upholstery, the device looked very much like a huge emperor scorpion. The user rested his head on this crown, to which electrodes were attached to communicate with the implant located in the user's brain.

Four chairs were arranged in an island, with the legs pointing towards the center. The room was decorated very simply, with concrete walls and nothing to hide the pipes in the ceiling. The subdued lighting gave the place a slightly gloomy air.

Laurent continued.

"The Metahub is a revolutionary new technology that connects most areas of the brain with the world of the Metaverse. The chair has interconnections that communicate directly with a brain implant. Thanks to this technology, people are literally immersed in the Metaverse, and their consciousness is connected in every way with the virtual world. They can see, hear, smell, touch and move in the Metaverse just as they would in the real world. The Metahub opens up new perspectives for experiencing unique and unimaginable emotions, impossible to experience in reality."

Lidia continued.

"I love Laurent's enthusiasm, but he didn't tell you everything. There's a price to pay for this total immersion in the Metaverse. Time spent in the Metaverse has consequences for users' mental and physical health. Some people become addicted to this virtual immersion and lose their link with the real world. Others suffer from psychological disorders such as depression and anxiety. All these considerations mean that the use of Metahub is highly controversial and used only by certain daring individuals, like us," she said more seriously.

"How do these devices work?"

Lidia hastened to answer.

"Metahubs are the ultimate interfaces between our minds and the Metaverse. The Metahub represents more than just a visual or auditory coupling like your Metabrain. It really allows you to embody yourself in the Metaverse. The Metahub excites the emotional zones of your brain so that you can feel and perceive the virtual world in the same way as the real universe."

Laurent added,

"This technology represents the most advanced known to date. However, it's very expensive. Minsky has one, too. I'll let Lidia continue, as this plan is pretty much her idea."

Lidia continued.

"We know that Minsky's oligarchs like to celebrate. So, we've created a brand-new, festive universe in the Metaverse, accessible only via the Metahub. This universe is only available to the VIPs of this world, as the fees are exorbitant. Virtual and erotic parties, a casino, and raves. Remember, Metahubs let you experience everything, as if you were there. We've designed extraordinary shows combining circus, wild animals and sexuality. Everything to satisfy the megalomaniacs of this society. The wealthy, like Minsky, have their own private league. We've invited some of our wealthy contributors for free to give the club notoriety, but most of the participants are AI-controlled avatars over whom we retain control and who serves as bait. After months of hype and social networking among our contributors, we managed to get dozens of these billionaires to join our club, including Minsky."

"How do you plan to approach him?" asked Jason.

"By passing yourself off as a new 'unicorn.' We'll assign you a fan club and invent a second life for you. Not so different from your own, just a little amplified. This way, we think we can confuse them with our game. Then Minsky will have no choice but to invite you into his VIP club, and you'll manage to get into his inner circle. It shouldn't be that difficult because we'll literally make you attractive. Afterwards, you'll try to contact Minsky."

"Am I going alone?"

"No," replied Laurent. "Lidia will accompany you. She'll keep an eye on you and let us know if anything goes wrong."

"Wrong! Can it be risky? You're not telling me everything."

"In fact, if they discover the trap, it won't be long before they disappear. However—"

"What?" asked Jason worried.

"Well, they may also decide to take immediate revenge and sequester you in the Metaverse."

Jason was feeling increasingly nervous.

"Sequestering in the Metaverse? How is this possible? What does this mean? I don't get it."

"Well, let's just say that certain members of the company have privileged access to the network of Metahubs. These privileges determine who enters and who leaves the Metaverse. These rights are generally managed by governments, but some influential people, like Minsky, have acquired these prerogatives, with, let's mention it, a few bank transfers from a few high-ranking officials. So, as I was saying, if they discover the scam, they might as well block your avatar in the Metaverse. And since your brain is directly connected to the Metaverse via your Metahub, you could get caught in."

"Forever? Can't you just disconnect me?"

"Unfortunately, no. This type of interface is so embedded in your brain cells that if we were to suddenly unplug you while you're in the Metaverse, it could have irreversible consequences for your mind. The only way out is to have access rights to the Metaverse. However, we don't know many people who would be willing to help us, given the nature of the mission and, above all, of the individuals involved. I hope you understand."

Lidia continued.

"You don't have to worry too much. So far, none of the club members suspect ownership. What's more, you'll have a certain notoriety with these billionaires. They won't be suspicious of anything."

Jason began to think of the disastrous consequences if he remained stuck in the Metaverse. He also thought of the impact if he didn't act. These oligarchs indirectly controlled the fate of the world. Through the nature of his business, he had met a few of them, who didn't seem so extreme in their positions. But he knew there were exceptions. If Minsky wasn't warned and, above all, convinced of the threats to EMA, the repercussions would be enormous, and they could kiss all our efforts to save Western society goodbye. The stakes were high. Time was running out. So, he made his decision.

"All right. I'm willing to take the risk."

"Excellent," replied Laurent. "We knew we could count on you. Now you need to get ready. First, we need to adapt your Metabrain interface to make it compatible with the Metahub. This will involve minor surgery. Since you already have an implant installed, it will be easier for us to do so. After a few hours' convalescence, to check that there are no complications and that the system is fully functional, we'll be able to send you on your way."

"In the meantime," continued Lidia, "we'll prepare your avenue by 'pimping' your profile in the Metaverse. We'll spread the word that a new investor, in this case Laurent, has just offered you several billion for your invention."

"I wish that were true."

"Don't worry," said Laurent, "we have the means to reward you in other ways."

Jason thought again of his father. He was beginning to realize the weight of this mission for the future of humankind. A burden he hoped he could bear.

Jason firmly believed that technology was the only way to safeguard the planet's integrity in the face of society's contradictions. Innovative projects like EMA and other clean energy technologies were the key to ensuring that everyone could continue to live in a free and prosperous society, without ruining the environment.

He was aware that his business project was only the first step in his career. He didn't expect his invention to revolutionize the world, but he hoped it would enable him to generate income quickly and finance his projects. His goal was to join the ranks of the wealthy, so that he could invest in technologies that would have a real impact on the development of societies. He knew this could be perceived as idealism, but he was inspired by individuals such as Minsky and, to some extent, Garnier, who had dared to think outside the box and propose concrete solutions to the problem of global warming. His ambition was to follow in their footsteps and actively contribute to a sustainable future.

Jason snapped out of his dream and asked Lidia:

"What's your character?"

"I'll be the new unicorn's girlfriend," she winked at Jason.

"Well, I guess that'll give you a privileged place in the unicorn kingdom!" Jason replied with a smile, appreciating Lidia's playful spirit.

Jason smiled proudly and Lidia noticed.

"Who knows, maybe we won't have to overplay our roles?" said Lidia.

"Maybe not," Jason finally replied.

Chapter 9

For the rest of the week, while the Möbius team planned the final details of the mission, Jason and Lidia had a *tête-à-tête* at *Chez Georges.*

Lidia began to tell him who she was and where she'd come from. She told him how, as a young girl, she had been struck by tragedy that left its mark on her vengeful character. At the time, her parents had lost their lives in a terrible rail accident. The derailment of the high-speed train was caused by an error in the AI-controlled steering system. Hundreds died as a result of the train's excessive speed. A public inquiry was held to determine responsibility and found that the AI had failed. However, the company that had designed the AI was cleared, which caused a scandal. Indeed, attributing responsibility to an artificial entity without human accountability had provoked strong reactions. This investigation served as the basis for the establishment of laws governing the involvement of AIs in this type of disaster.

Following this accident, which orphaned her, Lidia was raised by her grandparents. They held a special place in her heart. They had done everything in their power to give her a happy life and every possible opportunity. From an early age, they instilled in her, the importance of studying and succeeding at school.

But the trauma of losing her parents had affected her deeply, and she left school early, disgusted by the routine. She then went through a series of difficult experiences, working odd jobs and coming face to face with poverty and delinquency. This period hardened her and gave her a more realistic outlook on life. After a few years living as a fugitive, and tiring of this tumultuous existence, she rediscovered her determination and resumed her studies in artificial intelligence. She finally graduated with pride.

Today, she worked for Möbius, where she contributed with conviction to a just cause. This movement opposed companies and governments that failed to defend the interests of people and the environment. In Möbius, Lidia had found a cause close to her heart and a community that shared her values. She was ready to do anything to defend these unknown interests, including violent protest when necessary. Her determination and commitment were unshakable, and she was ready to pay the price for her own freedom and that of others. Her vengeful spirit had become an integral part of her being, inscribed in her DNA.

Looking thoughtful, Jason now had a better understanding of Lidia's motives. She noticed that he seemed troubled.

"How do you feel?" asked Lidia.

"In fact, this situation makes me a little ambivalent. On the one hand, I'm a bit shocked at the way you've lured me in with these stories about fake investors."

"I'm sorry, but we felt it was the only way to do it and get you to Paris. Especially after what you'd been through in Montreal during the bombing."

"On the other hand, the cause motivates me. The one that may involve the future of EMA. When you offered me the mission, I immediately thought of my father."

"What happened to him?"

Jason told Lidia about his father's tragic accident and his resentment of the inquest's findings.

"You know, the capabilities of AI are often exaggerated," continued Jason. "Despite all the achievements this technology has made in recent years, it is, in my opinion, no more intelligent than a lemur. To claim that AI is the cause of our problems is to shirk one's responsibilities."

"I understand you perfectly," remembering the tragic fate of his parents.

Lidia looked down, struggling to hold back her tears. Jason took her hand tenderly in his.

"I'm sorry," said Jason.

"It's not your fault. As with your father, the investigation also exonerated the company that designed the AI. This is absurd."

"What's absurd, in my opinion, is that these big companies don't respect their own code of ethics when pushing their AI-based applications. Their development teams sometimes turn corners so as not to jeopardize the release of this or that product. And the consequences can become disastrous, as you know."

"I confess. Ever since my parents died, I've sworn to denounce this kind of behavior. Did you know that Laurent's daughter was also the victim of an 'accident' caused by AI?"

"What? I'm sorry to hear that."

"His daughter was a collateral victim of an explosion at a chemical plant. She wasn't lucky enough to escape alive. How tragic."

Lidia and Jason's eyes met.

"Tell me more about Laurent's theory on the viruses that infect AIs. How do they work?"

"Well, as you know, AI systems are based on artificial neural networks, which are the mathematical representation of those found in our brains. Each artificial neuron can be connected to hundreds or even thousands of others. Once online, they possess properties similar to our memory."

Jason had already mastered all this, having studied in the field. But Lidia was so radiant when she spoke with passion that he didn't interrupt her so he could admire her.

"We program these 'memories' by training them in the same way as humans do. For example, if we want the AI to be able to recognize a 'cat,' we show it hundreds of images of cats. During its training, the AI learns to detect the cat's characteristic features. Muzzle, whiskers, ears and so on. Subsequently, the artificial memory can recall new cat images even if it hasn't seen them before.

"In addition to cats, an AI can be trained to drive a car, fly a plane or control a factory. AI training is based on human experience, which the AI learns to imitate. This is similar to the learning process in children, who observe and reproduce adult behaviors. Subsequently, the AI can operate autonomously without intervention. It can react to any situation it has assimilated during its training. It simply relies on algorithms and models to make decisions and act accordingly.

"Viruses can alter some of these memories in such a way as to modify the AI's behavior towards new events. These changes are subtle and difficult to detect, as an AI may have stored millions of these memories beforehand. What's more, some reminiscences can be interwoven and interrelated.

"When a particular situation arises, such as the presence of an animal on the road, or when a train starts to turn at high speed, the behavior induced in the AI, altered by the virus, is triggered, and an accident becomes inevitable."

"Why is it so difficult to detect this type of threat?" asked Jason.

"The virus attacks the AI's 'memories' by modifying just a few of the tens of millions of mathematical parameters it can contain. It only acts on a few of these parameters. It's imperative that the hackers know how the AI is programmed to make a small change that will become undetectable and, above all, won't affect the AI's normal reaction, so as not to raise any doubts. The virus will only modify one or two of the AI's behaviors, which in certain circumstances can be catastrophic."

Jason was familiar with this scheme, but he'd never imagined it was so complex to pull off. He understood why hackers resorted to this method. It allowed them to create considerable damage without being detected. A successful attack of this kind required in-depth expertise in the field of AI and precise knowledge of how the targeted AI worked. It was clear that the hackers behind this cyberattack were seasoned professionals, capable of exploiting the specific weaknesses and vulnerabilities of AI systems. Jason realized that the security of AI devices needed to be strengthened to counter such attacks and protect users from the harmful consequences of malicious AI exploitation.

"So, what you and Laurent are claiming is that foreign terrorist groups are spreading viruses in AI systems in order to modify some of these learned behaviors and cause impromptu 'accidents'?"

"Indeed, and even more worryingly, all the clues point to China. For several years now, China has been using its cyber-army to try and destabilize the West. All the ingredients are there for another world war to break out and wipe us all out."

"And what would their motives before these attacks?" asked Jason.

"China has been the world's biggest economic power since the '30s. Back then, they finally dethroned the Americans, who had dominated the planet since the second half of the twentieth century. Today, they see EMA as a threat to their hegemony. Minsky offered to integrate EMA into their economy, but they refused, seeing it as Western interference in their administration. The problem is that EMA operates mainly as a closed circuit, giving these belligerent countries virtually no opportunity to profit from the world market. All they want is to re-establish their ascendancy over the global economy. This is why they're prepared to use cyberterrorism tactics to achieve their goal. The only solution left to them is to destroy EMA and start again as before, when they dominated."

Lidia took a sip from her wine glass to catch her breath and continued.

"This could have catastrophic consequences for the entire planet, as EMA now exerts considerable influence on the global economy and the lives of billions of people. If EMA were to be wiped out, it could lead to the collapse of the Western economy, with appalling repercussions for the society as a whole."

"A crisis that would engender a recession and jeopardize all the efforts we've been making for years to save the planet from climate disaster," added Jason.

"There's no doubt about it. Worse, this would inevitably trigger an apocalyptic conflict between the West and China that could well be our ultimate quarrel."

Jason stared at Lidia for a long moment, absorbed by what she had just said. Was the end so near? Was he being too pessimistic about humanity's future?

However, he decided to take advantage of this little moment of happiness and kissed Lidia tenderly. Lidia smiled and took Jason by the hand.

Lidia walked Jason back to his hotel. Without saying a word, they both went up to his room. Jason had never before felt so moved. He didn't even think it was possible anymore.

Jason had been living alone for years. His existence was centered on his research and the company he had recently founded with his sister. He saw no room for sharing his life with anyone else. He sometimes found it futile to become emotionally attached to someone, knowing full well that he couldn't build a family, as current laws limited the number of births. The choice of forming a family had become so complicated that it discouraged many. Young adults had become accustomed to a lifestyle of temporary dating, with no commitment to each other.

But deep inside, Jason was feeling something new for the first time. Was it the fact that Lidia was intelligent and attractive, or was it the absurd situation of the mission that made him react differently? Whatever it was, he decided to give in to his emotions.

He felt like he was experiencing a new life. All the fears and uncertainties he'd had until then were gone. He felt at peace with himself and happy to be here, with Lidia. He lay down on the bed and hugged her.

Lidia smiled and kissed him tenderly.

Jason held him even tighter to show his affection.

They spent the night together, abandoning themselves to each other and loving each other without restraint, as if it were their last time.

Chapter 10

Jason gently opened his eyes, gradually recovering from the passionate night he'd had with Lidia. They then got ready to go to the Möbius premises, where he was to have his interface with the Metahub implanted.

The operation was quick, lasting just a few minutes. When he woke up, Jason still had a slight headache, no doubt due to the anesthetic he'd been given. His mouth was dry, a sure sign that he was thirsty after the operation. He resolved to drink copiously, in order to relieve the sensation and rehydrate adequately.

Laurent entered the recovery room to see Jason still bedridden.

"Everything's perfect," said Laurent. "The device has been installed and you'll be able to connect to the Metahub in a few hours. In the meantime, rest well. It's already been a busy day."

Jason closed his eyes and slept for a few hours.

When he woke up, Lidia was beside him with a radiant smile.

"Ready for the adventure of a lifetime?"

Jason was already feeling better. The effects of the anesthesia were slowly wearing off. He said to Lidia:

"I think my adrenalin level has gone up, because I feel unusually excited and nervous."

"It's normal, you've been given a little. You need to build up a lot of energy if you want to be persuasive in your role."

Jason remembered why he was here. He was beginning to feel the weight of the mission. Jason dozed off again, while Lydia held his hand.

A few hours later, Laurent entered the room.

"Ready for adventure? In fact, I envy you. Who wouldn't like to have a little fun in those VIP clubs? Life has become so gloomy lately."

"You can look at it that way, but I'm putting my life on the line in a way."

"It's either today or twenty years from now, when the Earth will have become uninhabitable. The choice is yours," he said wryly.

"So, when do we start so we can get it over with?" Jason retorted humorously.

"I like your attitude," Laurent laughed.

"Has the 'Unicorn Novel' been published yet?" asked Jason.

"Do you want to talk about your social networking profile? Yes, we do. We've posted hundreds of news posts on the networks announcing our new alliance. The impact is so enormous that I've already received calls from people who are genuinely interested in investing in your company. As I said, you'll still come out of this adventure with what you thought you'd get in the first place: financing for your business."

Laurent sensed that Jason was preoccupied.

"You seem anxious, don't you?" he said.

"I admit it. This is no ordinary mission."

"I'll give you that," said Laurent. "You know, there's still time to give it up. But before you make your decision, let me tell you something. A few years ago, I lost my daughter in one of those attacks—"

"Yes, I know. Lidia told me. I'm terribly sorry."

Laurent began to tell him how his princess had been killed in an accident that had claimed dozens of victims. That morning, his daughter went to school as usual. The route always took them close to the industrial district where a factory was located. Suddenly, a fire broke out in the benzene storage tanks. An explosion of unprecedented violence occurred, accompanied by a colossal flame rising dozens of meters into the air. A deafening noise echoed through the surrounding area. A crater over 120 meters in diameter and 1.6 meters deep formed, releasing a thick column of black smoke into the air.

The tragic death toll was 78, including firefighters and a large number of workers trapped when the factory collapsed. The search for survivors continued for several days in the rubble. Many residents were injured by flying glass, including 136 schoolchildren, among them Laurent's daughter. Sadly, she didn't survive, becoming a collateral victim of the tragedy.

On that fateful day, Laurent was out of town on business. His heart had been forever bruised when he heard the news in the Metaverse. In the months that followed, he isolated himself and fell into a deep depression.

All the clues pointed to criminal negligence, fueling public suspicion. The company was already tainted by a dark past. A few years earlier, the director and another executive had been arrested on suspicion of illegally burying hazardous waste in a communal landfill. Upon investigation, however, it was concluded that the error lay in the plant's AI-controlled management system. No charges were brought against the managers, prompting indignation, and also raising questions as to their responsibility for the incident.

Laurent was deeply skeptical about the findings of the investigation. As an expert in the field of AI, he knew full well that the systems controlling the operations of an automated factory were designed to prevent such incidents and guarantee the system's resilience in the face of the unexpected. He was convinced that criminal negligence on the part of those responsible for monitoring operations was at the root of the tragedy. In his opinion, if some efforts had been made to closely monitor the AI's actions, his daughter would never have lost her life.

In the depths of his depression, Laurent was approached by Möbius representatives. This opportunity enabled him to break out of his slump and turn his life towards a new goal. By joining Möbius, Laurent wanted to denounce our unquestioning dependence on AI, and, above all, the total abandonment and insouciance people had towards this technology.

He had quickly risen through the ranks of the organization, thanks to his skills, wealth, and boundless determination. In just a few months, he was appointed Director of Operations for the Paris chapter. This promotion gave him a key role in the implementation of Möbius's actions, and a platform to put forward his ideas and convictions. Armed with his position, Laurent was determined to put in place concrete initiatives to promote the organization's values and advance its mission of defending the environment and social justice.

He wanted to raise public awareness of the dangers of this excessive dependence, and to promote the introduction of control measures to oversee the use of these technologies. He saw this situation as an opportunity to militate in favor of these causes and contribute to a more responsible and balanced world. For Laurent, it was undeniable that AI had immense potential to improve our lives, but it was equally crucial not to let it become a tyrant. He wanted Möbius to set an example, showing that it was possible to create intelligent technologies without endangering humanity.

"The recent attacks have made me realize just how much importance we attribute to artificial intelligence these days," said Laurent. "We've become accustomed to just relying on AI, to drive our cars, to fly our planes and even to manage our lives. It has replaced radiologists, lawyers and, in a way, journalists. AI has become such an indispensable commodity, on a par with running water or electricity, that we no longer question how it works or its purpose. It's too often used to replace humans, rather than to assist them. This seems to me to be a monumental mistake. In my opinion, we're heading for disaster if we let AI dominate us."

"Yes, but sometimes AI really does become essential and irreplaceable," said Jason. "Take EMA, for example. No one can match it in its titanic task."

"I don't quite agree with you. Granted, by eliminating the human from the decision-making loop, EMA makes its economic system more resilient and responsive to change. But how do we know that EMA's decisions are always in our favor?

EMA doesn't understand all the stakes its choices have on our society, because it doesn't have a clear idea of them. It has its limits, and it's only by putting people back into the loop that we'll be able to trust EMA. For EMA's business model to spread worldwide, it's essential to achieve widespread social acceptability."

Laurent lowered his tone and put his hand on Jason's shoulder. Jason looked away, a little thoughtful.

"In short, what I'm trying to say," continued Laurent, "is that, despite our different points of view on EMA, our objective is the same: to save the planet. I hope you understand. All I ask is that you think about our common goal, not our differences. This is paramount to the success of this mission. So, I ask you again: are you still willing to help us?"

Jason knew he had to try, even if the chances of success seemed slim. He thought again of his father. He hesitated briefly before asking Laurent:

"May I ask you a question before answering?"

"Certainly."

"Why do you dislike Minsky so much?"

"Because he's a despicable, unscrupulous being."

"You're exaggerating."

"Not at all. You've probably heard about that 'historic' conference at the United Nations, where everyone learned about EMA. Minsky recounts that all governments subsequently lined up to join EMA. It can't be that far from the truth. In fact, EMA's replacement of the world economy is the result of a series of corruptions, schemes and even tampering."

"Isn't that pushing it a bit far? I can believe that some civil servants and politicians may have been rotten but accusing him of terrorism is a bit of an exaggeration."

"Think again. Let me tell you a story that our journalists have brought to light. You've probably heard about the integration of France's economic administration with that of EMA. At the time, the President of France invited Minsky to talk to his cabinet and explain the advantages of cryptonomy. Some, like the French Finance Minister, weren't convinced of the benefits of integration. However, a series of industrial accidents, caused by faulty AI control systems, sounded the death knell for the French economy, which was already struggling due to the dominance of China. The country was on the verge of bankruptcy. Minsky was immediately seen as a savior, and the adoption of EMA enabled France to start afresh and rebuild its economy. The National Assembly even amended the constitution to incorporate EMA into its laws. The President was also found to have received large sums of money from Minsky, following this crucial legal step. Minsky repeated this same ploy in numerous countries. So, you see, my dear friend, this man isn't what he claims to be. He has his own interests at heart above all else."

"In a way, China is trying to destabilize the EMA economy, just as Minsky did for the world economy."

"You're absolutely right. However, the consequences of this conflict may have more significant repercussions, because, in addition to being an economic superpower, China is a military one, which wasn't the case for Minsky."

"Tell me," asked Jason, "when you were talking about industrial accidents caused by Minsky, did any of them have anything to do with your daughter's death?"

Laurent didn't answer for a few seconds, as emotion muzzled him. After a moment, he replied.

"We don't have proof beyond doubt, but events suggest that this is the case. Now you can see why I feel so strongly about Minsky. But anyway, it's important now to think about the future. Are you ready to follow us, Jason?"

"I think so."

"Excellent! Let's go now," said Laurent.

Laurent, Lidia and Jason then headed for the great hall where the Metahubs were located, the armchairs that served as portals to the Metaverse.

"Please, sit down," said Laurent.

Lidia and Jason sat side by side on their seat. Lidia extended her hand to Jason's, who grasped it firmly. She smiled at him, and he smiled back. Near their heads, the technicians adjusted the electronic crown that served as an interface between the implants and the Metaverse. Jason felt a small pain in his hypodermis, as if an electric wire had been connected. Once contact had been established, the two automatically fell into darkness.

Chapter 11

Jason awoke a few moments later, feeling strangely out of place in his own body. A strange sensation came over him as he looked down at his hands and arms, noticing that he was wearing a bright purple jacket and beige leather shoes with pointed toes, reminiscent of the style of medieval troubadours. On his head was a hunting hat, embellished with a long pheasant feather. Observing his surroundings, he spotted Lidia beside him, dressed in a sumptuous purple evening gown with a plunging neckline down to her hips. Her meticulous makeup and pumps gave her an undeniable elegance.

"I suppose you're the one who selected our costumes," asserted Jason.

"Yes, indeed," laughed Lidia. "As you'll have gathered, my favorite color is purple."

Jason stood up and approached the wall of the bubble. He touched it with his fingertips and felt it strangely warm and elastic.

"Where are we?" he asked.

"We've arrived in what's known as the welcome bubble to familiarize you with our world."

"It's incredible," retorted Jason. "It's like we're floating in some kind of giant jar."

Jason continued to look around him. The room he had entered was in fact a huge transparent bubble. A balloon that seemed to float in an ocean. Outside, Jason saw thousands of multicolored fish, larger ones, sharks and even whales. He noticed a strange animal that looked like a dinosaur.

"It's a shastasaurus," anticipated Lidia. "One of the most enormous marine dinosaurs that ever lived on earth. That's the beauty of the virtual world. You can invent the world you want and even bring back to life what no longer exists."

"Fascinating!" said Jason, following the dinosaur with his eyes.

Jason spotted another bubble approaching in the distance. He saw people waving at him. Lidia explained.

"Our club is made up of several bubbles, in which we imagined different themes. We wanted to reproduce the concept of bubbles in an ocean of champagne. Some offer live entertainment, while others offer games of chance."

"How do I access another bubble?"

"It's easy. In a virtual world, you can either walk normally or teleport. To do so, point your finger in the direction you want to go, and you'll be teleported there automatically. Try it and see."

Jason then pointed in one direction and a curved beam of light shot out from his index finger, falling to the ground some distance away. After three seconds, he spontaneously found himself in the target location.

"If you want to move to another bubble, just point with your finger and you'll be teleported there automatically."

"What happens if I point outside a bubble, in the ocean, for example? Could I drown?"

"Not at all. In the virtual world, you don't really breathe. You just feel a little wet, that's all," she laughed.

Lidia continued.

"If you're ready, we'll teleport to the next bubble. Expect a welcoming committee because we've announced your arrival. Ready?"

"Yes."

"Oh yes, before I forget, don't be fooled by the appearance of everyone's avatar. Most people don't use a character designed in their own image. They use more flattering representations of themselves. Some of the people you'll meet are in their eighties, even though their avatars look much younger."

"Why didn't you use a different avatar to personify us?" asked Jason.

"I didn't see the relevance. The others must recognize you if they're to be confused."

Lidia continued.

"We're going to the bubble called 'Club EMA.' This is where Minsky and his supporters meet. You're expected there."

Lidia pointed at a bubble and moved it into Jason's field of vision. Lidia and Jason then pointed to a nearby bubble. Three seconds later, they found themselves surrounded by a small reception committee.

Chapter 12

Dozens of people greeted Jason and Lidia. All were dressed in elegant suits and wore affable smiles. Two of them approached Jason and extended their hands.

"Welcome, my dear. We've been looking forward to meeting you."

The two men, who looked quite young—although Jason knew they were most likely much older in the real world—were disguised as astronauts from the early space age.

"I'm Neil Armstrong and he's Buzz Aldrin," smiled one of the individuals.

"Pleased to meet you," said a bewildered Jason, searching Lidia's face with his gaze.

"Oh, yes, I forgot to tell you that nobody here uses their real name. It's up to you," replied Lidia.

Jason hesitated a little before replying, "Holmes, Sherlock Holmes."

"Delighted, Mr. Holmes," they said.

"Buzz and I have been hearing a lot about you lately."

"For the better, I hope?"

"Absolutely. We're convinced that your invention would be an invaluable addition to the EMA ecosystem, because it's indeed a digital ecosystem that must be built around EMA. Without its partners, EMA would be an empty brain."

Buzz continued.

"For example, Neil and I have set up a fully automated robotic delivery system that takes products from factory gates and delivers them to consumers with little or no human intervention. A supply chain that integrates fleets of autonomous trucks and ships with flying and walking robots and drop parcels off at your front door. Our platform is fully grafted and controlled by EMA, which optimizes the entire process in real time to minimize the ecological footprint associated with transport."

"Wonderful," said Jason. "How do you think my invention can help you?"

"We have our idea, but it would be best if you could meet Minsky to discuss it. Unfortunately, he hasn't arrived yet, but he shouldn't be long. In the meantime, help yourself to the bar and relax. We'll forward him the message."

"Thank you."

Lidia and Jason went to the counter and ordered cocktails. They were served glasses containing a brightly colored liquid they could hardly identify. They savored it.

"Yeah, mine tastes like a Margarita, just the way I like them."

"Mine tastes of white wine. Very pleasant indeed."

"In fact, you can change the flavor of drinks just by thinking about it for a few seconds. Give it a try."

Jason imagined a single malt scotch and took another sip. The taste had in fact changed, from white wine to scotch. Wonderful.

Jason then asked Lidia:

"Who were these two 'astronauts'?"

"Don't you recognize them? They're the Smith brothers, who developed the concept of the physical Internet for the supply chain. They own an immense fortune and are well into their eighties. Nothing to do with these avatars."

"The Smith brothers?"

"Jason couldn't believe he'd met these two legends."

"What exactly is the physical Internet," asked Jason?

"Imagine a global freight transport system operating like the Internet. Cargoes are transported in standardized parcels or containers, while the autonomous network analyzes data in real time to determine the best route and most efficient mode of transport. This system optimizes product distribution, reduces unnecessary travel and minimizes environmental costs. Thanks to this approach, good delivery becomes smoother, more economical and more respectful of the environment."

"Hence the link with EMA. Optimization means EMA."

"You've got it."

Lidia and Jason moved to the couches near the bar.

Jason looked a little worried.

"What's wrong?" asked Lidia.

"I'm worried about my meeting with Minsky. I wouldn't want him to find out that I'm associated with your group and ensnare me."

"Don't worry, our people keep a close eye on your vital signs. As soon as they see something suspicious, they'll get you out of there."

They continued to discuss their project for a few minutes, until a man approached them. It was Minsky. He was tall and imposing, with long gray hair and a neat beard. He looked intelligent and confident, as if he was used to making important decisions.

"Hello, Mr. Webb, it's a pleasure to meet you."

"Holmes, Sherlock Holmes," Jason smiled.

"Of course, but I prefer to be transparent and not hide anything. These stupid names irritate me a little."

"No doubt," said Jason, a little embarrassed.

"And you are?" he said, taking Lidia's hand to kiss it.

"Marilyn Monroe, I accompany Sherlock. But you can call me Lidia."

"Pleased to meet you," said Minsky.

"My friends over there told me I might be interested in your invention. Could you tell me a little more about it?"

Jason knew this was his moment to take center stage. He launched enthusiastically into his sales pitch.

"In fact, we've developed a concept to ensure the traceability of products and food, wherever they may be. Basically, it's a new, inert molecule that can be integrated into almost anything. A code specific to each molecule and each commodity enables it to be recognized. The code can be deciphered to identify the commodity's origin at any time, thanks to simple spectrometric devices and AI. What's more, as each molecule is made up of certain atoms with a known half-life, we can measure how long the product has been in production. These molecules act as a label and a clock, integrated into each good.

"This allows consumers to know where the goods come from and how long they've been on the market. This information is vital in the agricultural and food sectors, where freshness and quality are crucial. It can also be applied to manufactured goods, to find out where they come from and whether they have been produced under favorable ethical and ecological conditions. Finally, this technology could also be used to combat counterfeiting and guarantee the authenticity of goods."

"Very interesting, Mr. Webb. In fact, your solution could meet an essential need for EMA. Because, as you can imagine, EMA needs to know at all times where and when a given product is located. This is essential if it's to make the best decision for its economy. If certain goods find their way into the environment, EMA will immediately take the appropriate measures to prevent pollution. Taking care of nature is also part of its mission, you know."

Minsky continued.

"You know, Mr. Webb, EMA wasn't just designed to save our planet. Above all, it was designed to divert men from their incompetence. For centuries, we've entrusted control of our lives to shameless entrepreneurs whose sole concern was the accumulation of indecent wealth. It's better to have an objective, infallible AI than one of these economic puppeteers managing the lives of billions of people. That's why I'm devoting my heart and soul to the complete realization of EMA, even if it's to the detriment of my opponents."

Jason and Lidia were taken aback by Minsky's reactionary attitude. However, anxious not to offend him, they avoided contradicting him. Instead, Jason decided to go ahead with his idea.

"I'm glad to hear it, sir. Minsky. It shows that your solution meets a concrete and important need for humankind. We look forward to working with you, but first we'd like to discuss another topic with you."

The conversation was interrupted by another man whispering something in Minsky's ear.

Minsky turned back to Jason, smiling less.

"Mr. Webb, sorry but we will have to talk about this later. I'm sorry to have to leave you, but something came up at the last minute. To continue our discussion, I invite you to my home in California next week. My intelligent personal assistant will get in touch with you."

"It's no problem at all. I understand."

"Perfect. Until next time!"

Minsky then stood up and, with a snap of his fingers, suddenly disappeared.

Lidia and Jason were left a little shaken by what had just happened. They wondered why Minsky's mood had suddenly changed. Had he discovered their strategy?

"I don't think we need to worry," said Lidia. "If they'd known our real intentions, they'd have blocked us in the Metaverse. That kind of person has no remorse. But to be on the safe side, we need to get out of here before things get ugly."

The next second, everything went black. Jason opened his eyes again, sitting in the Metahub in the Möbius room. Laurent remained standing beside him.

"What do you think?" Jason asked Laurent.

"I don't know. In principle, our presence is almost undetectable. But Minsky has resources that most people don't have. Not even the French army. I think it's safe to accept his offer to meet him at his house. We need to find out more."

For the first time, Jason was afraid. A fear with no real basis, but a fear, nonetheless. Fear of failing and, above all, of sacrificing all the work he'd been doing for years.

He took a deep breath and tried to relax. He reminded himself that every project involves risk, and that he had to face his fears and keep moving forward. He told himself that he'd worked too hard to give up now, and that Minsky had faith in him. He got up and prepared to leave for California, determined to succeed in his mission.

Chapter 13

Jason was still stunned by the whole experience. His mind was also electrified by his encounter with Minsky and the excess adrenalin coursing through his veins. The experience had opened his eyes to a new perspective on Minsky, quite different from what he had originally believed. He now realized that this character wasn't just an idealist, but also concealed a malicious ambition. This revelation disturbed him to the core, calling into question his confidence and beliefs. He now wondered what Minsky's true motives and objectives were, and how this might affect the world around them.

Laurent advised him to rest before planning their next meeting in California. He said he needed to relax before making any definitive decisions.

He asked Sherlock to hail him a self-driving cab back to his hotel. After dictating his destination to the cab's console, he settled comfortably into the back seat and lay down on his side, exhausted by so many emotions.

The vehicle then moved off and entered the traffic, which was light at this late hour. Jason let his thoughts wander as he recalled the events of the past day. He remembered the cavalier way in which Minsky had bailed, leaving doubts about his true intentions. Had he been warned of Minsky's true intentions before the meeting? Was it a trick invitation, or did he really want to learn more about his invention? These questions swirled around and around in Jason's mind, fueling his suspicion and his desire to find out more about Minsky's true motives.

As he drove down the road, Jason noticed that the cab was heading in a direction that took him away from his original destination. A feeling of suspicion took hold of him. Suddenly, the vehicle accelerated sharply, narrowly avoiding other cars and pedestrians in its path. The speed increased alarmingly, and Jason could feel his heart beating faster and faster. He wondered what was happening and tried to find an explanation for this unexpected situation.

Then he realized that the vehicle's navigation system had lost all control. Panic gripped him as he watched in horror as the cab approached a bridge over the Seine.

"Help me, Sherlock! What can I do?"

"Press the red button near the left door," said Sherlock calmly.

He spotted an emergency stop button near the door and leaned desperately to reach it. However, despite his many attempts, the button seemed defective and refused to respond. The violent jolts caused by the cab rolling along the sidewalk threw him from one side of the cab to the other, leaving him disoriented and vulnerable. In a growing state of panic, he shouted frantically for the vehicle to stop, but his pleas seemed to get lost in the chaos of the situation.

The cab abruptly turned off the road and continued its mad dash through a park bordering the Seine. Despite its breakneck speed, the vehicle surprisingly managed to avoid the obstacles in its path, narrowly missing the park benches and bushes. The anti-collision system seemed to be still operational, which further amplified the unreal sensation of the situation. Jason was desperately trying to find a solution, looking for a way to put an end to the crazy race that was threatening him.

However, the autonomous cab's system didn't seem to recognize the large tree in front of it. Instead of avoiding it, the vehicle kept heading straight for him, showing no sign of slowing down. Jason realized that this could be the end. Panicking, he tried desperately to get out of the car, but all the exits were blocked. He pounded ruthlessly on windows and doors, desperate to find a way out, but nothing seemed to give way. He felt completely trapped and powerless.

Suddenly, a beggar passed between the tree and the cab. The poor man, seeing the impending disaster, froze in place like an animal frightened at night by the headlights. Sensing this new situation, the vehicle changed direction and turned sharply to the right. It slammed hard into the stone railing along the riverbank. This took Jason's breath away. After a few seconds of precarious balance, the vehicle tipped towards the surface of the water. Jason tried to brace himself against the fall, but in vain.

The impact of the waves was brutal, shaking Jason violently inside the cab. Fortunately, he wasn't seriously injured. As the water began to fill the cab, the car began its descent into the depths of the Seine. Jason, in panic, tried desperately to open the door and window, but they remained stubbornly locked, preventing him from escaping. Despite his best efforts, he found himself trapped in this steel cage, which was sure to sink into the dark waters.

Struggling against the pressure of the water around him, Jason tried to keep calm. He recalled the instructions for survival in the event of drowning, trying to rationalize the situation. Minutes seemed to go on forever as the cab continued to sink into the depths of the Seine.

Water continued to accumulate in the cabin, and the vehicle sank inexorably into the bed of the Seine. Jason had just enough time to warn Sherlock to contact the emergency services, before he was submerged.

He managed to take one last breath of air before the waves covered him completely. He heard the sound of sirens and the cries of those who had witnessed the scene, muffled by the river. He tried to resist as long as he could, but after a few seconds he inevitably swallowed the water in his lungs. He felt an intense burning in his chest. He then lost consciousness and plunged again, into the blackness as if he'd fallen into the Metaverse. Deadly blackness for good.

Chapter 14

Jason slowly opened his eyes, his vision still blurred by the effects of the anesthetic. He felt a stabbing pain in his chest with every breath he took. Looking around, he noticed the many medical devices that were connected to him. Monitors flashed, displaying his vital signs, and doctors and nurses bustled around him.

The nurse was busy beside his bed, adjusting his solute. She smiled at him when she saw his eyes widen.

"Good morning, Mr. Webb! How are you?"

Jason's mouth was dry and pasty, an unpleasant sensation that made him intensely thirsty. He instinctively reached for a glass of water nearby, but immediately realized that he was still hooked up to the medical equipment and couldn't move freely.

"I'm OK," he said weakly.

"The paramedics rescued you in time. They were able to resuscitate you quickly, avoiding any after-effects. According to the doctor, you have a few bruises, but nothing serious. You'll be able to leave the hospital in just a few days," she added.

Jason tried to sit up in bed. His aching muscles reminded him of the terrible accident he had just suffered.

At the same moment, Lidia and Laurent entered the room.

"Jason, thank God you're OK," said Lidia.

She ran to his bedside and kissed him.

"You can say you've had a narrow escape," said Laurent.

"What happened?" asked Jason.

"You've been the victim of a cyberattack," said Lidia.

"By whom? ... I don't understand."

"According to our investigators, a cyber hacker from China carried out the attack. They succeeded in infecting the AI of the autonomous car," said Laurent. "What do you remember, Jason?"

"I was sitting comfortably in the cab, enjoying the ride, when suddenly the vehicle sped up. I could feel that something was wrong. The vehicle deftly dodged all obstacles in its path, but I was coming dangerously close to an imposing tree in a park along the Seine. Just when I thought the impact was inevitable, a person appeared out of nowhere, standing between the cab and the tree. The vehicle then unexpectedly changed direction, heading for the riverbank.

"I plunged several meters before hitting the water's surface. The impact was violent, but I was still aware of what was happening. I tried to get out of the cab, but in vain. Everything was blocked. I tried to call for help before the water flooded the cab. After that, I don't remember a thing."

"Your distress message was transmitted in time, and fortunately the rescuers came quickly enough to get you out of there," said Laurent.

Lidia stroked Jason's hair tenderly, smiling at him. Laurent continued.

"Based on our investigation, we believe that this provoked accident was aimed at deliberately eliminating you, probably because of your encounter with Minsky."

"But how did they know I'd joined? Didn't you tell me that your private club was under your control?"

"That's true. But we can't verify who Minsky invites. It's possible that he was followed by a traitor who passed on information to the enemy. This is probably linked to the leak of EMA secrets to China. The Chinese authorities are ruthless and act without scruples."

"Why did the autonomous cab suddenly change direction and not run into the tree to kill me?" asked Jason.

"We believe it was precisely programmed not to recognize the tree as an obstacle to be dodged. When the person stood between them, the AI saw that the target had changed and had no choice but to avoid the passer-by. As it had no room to maneuver in the direction it had chosen, the impact with the railing was inevitable. The authors of this virus couldn't have foreseen this situation. They hadn't modified the navigation program to take account of this fortuitous sequence of events."

"I've had a narrow escape, as you put it," said Jason. "But what adventure have I embarked upon?"

"I know what we're asking you to do is very risky and dangerous. But the stakes are too high for you to give up now. Western countries are on alert, and their governments are discussing major retaliatory measures. You must go and meet Minsky and warn him, it's urgent."

Lidia gave him an incensed look in response, letting him know that she disapproved of his harsh words. Laurent felt uncomfortable and hurried to catch up.

"But if you decide to stop there, I'll understand, too. The choice is yours."

Jason fell deep in its thought. He'd just experienced two dramatic attacks in less than a week, and he wasn't prepared for this kind of adventure. But he knew that if he didn't warn Minsky, the Chinese could do enormous damage to the world economy. He was sure of it. After a few seconds' thought, he turned to Laurent.

"Give me time to recover, and I'll give you an answer later."

"Understood," said Laurent.

"I'll stay with you for a while, Jason," said Lidia, stroking his hand, "and let you rest afterwards."

Jason closed his eyes and let the day's events run through his mind. Despite the pain that still coursed through him and the perilous situations he'd been in, he knew the story was far from over. He sensed that something, greater was on the horizon, but he couldn't yet imagine what lay ahead.

Chapter 15

A few days after his accident, Jason left the hospital and returned to his hotel. A little later, he joined his friend Étienne at *Chez Georges* bar.

"How are you?" asked Étienne, slightly worried when he saw his friend again, looking downcast.

"If you only knew, my friend."

"Tell me about it! Good Lord!"

Jason knew he could trust Étienne. He was his best friend, and he knew him very well. He couldn't imagine Étienne betraying him.

"Just imagine, I've met Minsky."

"What? But that's great! Wasn't it your dream to meet him? Did you tell him about your project?"

"In fact, I was approached by Möbius and—"

"Are you out of your mind?" Étienne shouted. "You can't trust this group of degenerates. They're a real danger, you know."

"Listen, strange things are happening on the Metaverse. EMA is facing an imminent threat, jeopardizing the economy of the entire West. The Chinese are being singled out for significant blame. The events underway could potentially lead to global repercussions, even triggering another war. In short, it caught my attention."

"For God's sake, Webb, it's not your job to fix the world. You've already got enough on your shoulders. You mustn't fall for these extremists."

"Perhaps you're right. I think I was attracted by the fact that it gave me an opportunity to avenge my father's death ... and also to meet Minsky, I must admit. And then the accident happened—"

"What's all this about?" he shouted.

"Now, calm down. I'll tell you everything."

"Tell me what happened, and quick."

"Basically, well, we went to join Minsky in the Metaverse. In a VIP club created and controlled by Möbius."

"How did you get there? Don't tell me you used Metahubs?"

"Yes," said Jason, lowering his head slightly, a little ashamed.

"Damn it, Webb! You know very well that you're now on file and connected to those bastards. They'll be able to access your every move and keep track of you. You're their pawn now."

"I know, I know. I didn't think of it at the time. But this thing doesn't come off, does it?"

"But no, that's just it. It's like a tattoo imprinted on your brain. It can't be removed without damaging your little head. You're connected for the rest of your life."

Jason suddenly felt sad and hopeless. He doubted everything. Étienne put a hand on his shoulder and spoke in a more soothing voice.

"Listen, my friend. It's not that bad. Many people tell their entire lives in Metaverse. And it's all accessible to anyone with a little curiosity. In your case, at least you'll be aware of who knows what you're saying or doing."

"Small consolation."

"Anyway, how did your interview with Minsky, end? Did you tell him about your suspicions about EMA's integrity?"

"We didn't really have time. As soon as we managed to meet him, one of his henchmen informed him of something. I don't know what, but it seemed to upset him. He then invited us to continue the conversation at his home in California next week."

"And you mentioned an accident? What happened?"

"At the end of our interview, I wanted to go to my room to rest. I took a cab. After a few minutes, it lost control completely and drove straight into a tree. At the last minute, someone stepped in between the vehicle and the tree, and the car suddenly turned towards the river. The vehicle fell into the water, and I lost consciousness. I woke up a few hours later in the hospital, saved by the paramedics."

"Good grief, Jason. Do you know why the cab malfunctioned?"

"According to Möbius, this was an attack by China to eliminate me. Somehow, they knew about my meeting with Minsky."

"After all this, are you still planning to meet Minsky in California?"

"I don't know, and that's why I wanted to talk to you."

"Listen, my friend. I've known you too long to think you're a stubborn person who wants to get to the bottom of things.

But stop thinking about saving the world and start thinking about yourself. Yes, I know the universe is short of heroes, but heroes didn't save us from the climate crisis. I'm sorry to say it like this, but in the history of humankind, very few serious events have been resolved solely by one individual. You don't have to be ashamed of abandoning them now."

After a long moment of silence, Jason looked up at Étienne.

"Actually, I don't really care about the accident. The evidence they presented to me was quite disturbing. Unscrupulous countries are behind the attacks. Their next target is EMA, and we need to warn Minsky."

"Are you annoyed because the hero you worship is no longer infallible? Or is it because the consequences of these attacks can be truly catastrophic?"

"It's true that my ideal is a little shaken. But I have the feeling that someone has managed to take EMA's computer control systems hostage and is starting to cause chaos. I don't know how or why, but I'd like to know more. The Möbius people are right. I'm in a very good position to try to contact Minsky and talk to him about this problem. So far, he's turned a deaf ear because he doesn't trust Möbius."

Jason rubbed his face between his hands, as if trying to mix his ideas.

"History has also shown us," continued Jason, "that in major crises such as pandemics and wars, an individual's action can make a huge difference if it's part of an overall goal. Many people often say that they can't do anything about climate change and that their individual actions don't count in the overall scheme of things. However, they fail to understand that we're all part of a global system, and that each personal act has an impact on the whole system, even if the consequences aren't immediately apparent."

Jason paused before continuing.

"You know, my grandparents lived through periods of pandemics in the '20s. A difficult time, which they told me about several times. My grandfather told me that many people thought there was no point in fighting the virus. They implored individual freedom at the expense of collective well-being. In short, if we'd listened to them, we might not be here having this conversation. It's thanks to seemingly inconsequential personal actions that we've been able to get through these crises."

"Today, we're once again faced with a problem that not only threatens our climate, but also the survival of our species. I know that my intervention with Minsky may not help, but I must try in the name of collective benefit."

"Maybe you're right," said Étienne. "Just take care of yourself. If you're going to be a hero, make sure you stay alive. I don't know many people who've become role models after their death," he said with a half-smile.

"Understood, my friend. I promise."

Jason pondered his words. Despite his certainty that he was doing the right thing, he still felt a palpable tension tickling his insides.

Chapter 16

Lidia savored her cocktail in the comfort of her first-class seat. Minsky had taken care to reserve a private jet for Jason and Lidia, offering them an exclusive and rapid trip. The hypersonic flight from Paris to San Francisco would take just a few hours, with a stopover in New York. Thanks to Minsky's intelligent assistant, everything was planned and organized, offering his lovebirds an all-inclusive travel experience.

The private jet was equipped with every possible amenity, including a lounge, bedroom and even a shower. Lidia and Jason had spent the flight discussing their project and their future collaboration with Minsky. They had also taken the opportunity to rest and relax after the stressful events of the last few days.

The plane began its descent.

"Let's review our strategy once more," said Lidia.

"I know," said Jason, a little annoyed. "We meet Minsky, tell him about my invention, then start talking about the bombings. Nothing too complicated."

"Yes, and we absolutely mustn't let him suspect we're Möbius. Don't even mention it. He'd arrest us on the spot. You know as well as I do that, he's terribly angry with us."

"Tell me, Lidia, why do you seem so angry with Minsky?"

"Because he's a vile, dishonest being and I have a deep aversion to that kind of guy."

"Why did he do to you?"

"You know as well as me, he doesn't hesitate to manipulate people to achieve his ends."

"Couldn't we be talking about influence rather than machinations?"

"What do you call a guy who literally sabotages companies to force them into the EMA economy? Minsky has become immensely wealthy thanks to his invention. His wealth is so colossal that it's impossible to conceive of its magnitude. He's richer than most countries in the world. And what does he do with his money? Nothing, really. Not even paying his taxes. Some states offer him tailor-made tax privileges."

"But he has also set up several foundations to help the underprivileged. He has also founded an institution to preserve biodiversity by acquiring protected areas."

"Hell no," she retorted, exasperated. "He's a megalomaniac who squanders his money to create private paradises for his friends. He even bought land on the moon so he could afford space travel. Those aren't protected areas, as far as I know. It gives him a place to take refuge in case of climatic catastrophes. As he well knows, EMA won't be able to solve all the problems. The environmental crisis will continue, and the population will suffer. And he will be wisely preserved in his 'areas,' as you put it."

"I see that I won't be able to change your point of view."

"Certainly not," she said, smiling mischievously at him.

The plane landed smoothly on the runway, the hypersonic engines making a shriller and more intense noise than the new electric turbines, but the aircraft's performance was remarkable.

"Head for the exit," said Sherlock, "a white limousine will be waiting for you."

As they exit the airport, he saw a long autonomous vehicle honking at them. It was waiting to take them to Minsky's luxurious villa. Inside, soft, enchanting music greeted them. Once settled, the limousine doors closed and a pleasant, feminine voice rang out: "Welcome to San Francisco. Please relax. You'll arrive at your destination in less than thirty minutes."

The "limo" took to the reserved lanes for autonomous vehicles, while Jason observed the rare paths still used by traditional automobiles, jammed with traffic.

It was his first visit to California. Along the way, he spotted iconic buildings such as Apple Park, the former headquarters of Apple, and the prestigious Stanford University, where Minsky and other famous figures had studied. These sites were symbols of the innovation and technology that characterized the Silicon Valley region.

The vehicle then turned into an upscale residential area of San Jose and drove for a few kilometers before slowing down in front of an iron gate. It opened automatically as the limousine approached. The vehicle stopped a few dozen meters in front of Minsky's residence.

His residence was in fact a gigantic British-style castle from the 18^{e} century, a copy of a stately home in Scotland. Minsky was a fan of the old series about the now-defunct British monarchy. Minsky's mansion was flanked by two side wings, which served as quarters for his staff. The facade was adorned with numerous dormer windows and turrets. A large park stretched out behind the mansion, with an immense lawn, formal gardens and a lake with a small bridge. The parterre was surrounded by a high wrought-iron gate, with a massive wooden main portal. Minsky's villa was a true haven of peace, a place where he could recharge his batteries and work in complete tranquility.

The vehicle's doors opened after it had come to a halt. At the entrance, Minsky welcomed them with open arms. Next to him, a row of individuals, probably castle staff, stood at attention. Their uniforms were both modern and stamped with a certain retro style, evoking bygone eras.

"Welcome to my home," Minsky smiled. "I hope you had a nice trip?"

"Excellent," replied Jason.

Jason noticed security guards all around the house. He thought it odd that there were so many.

Lidia and Jason followed Minsky inside.

Although the exterior of the manor house bore a striking resemblance to a traditional British castle, the interior was strikingly modern. Curved lines dominated, evoking nature in all its aspects. The decor was strongly inspired by Antoni Gaudí, the 19th-century Spanish architect who used color, texture and form in innovative ways. A central spiral staircase rose majestically to the upper floors, recalling the silhouette of a bean plant. Floors and walls were adorned with multicolored mosaics, while furniture, sculpted with flowing lines, seemed to take shape in the sand. Everything in this interior evoked nature, but a nature mastered and transformed by art and creativity.

The living room, located near the entrance, was one of the most remarkable areas of the house. The huge floor-to-ceiling windows offered a breathtaking view of the lush gardens. The walls were covered with mirrors that reflected each other, creating an illusion of infinity in space. A majestic grand piano sat at the center of the room, surrounded by elegantly arranged armchairs and comfortable sofas. Modern artworks, paintings and sculptures adorned the walls and shelves, adding a touch of sophistication to the whole. Every corner of the living room was carefully maintained and organized, giving the impression that the house was always ready to receive guests.

Lidia and Jason followed Minsky to what appeared to be his office. Minsky's desk was made from a large, giant California pine, giving the impression that the tree had grown directly into the room. Minsky offered them a seat on one of the couches while he stood in front of them.

Minsky was an imposing man, not for his size, but for the energy he exuded. His steel-gray hair was slicked back, revealing a face weathered by time and hard work. His thin beard was neatly trimmed. He had intense blue eyes that could pierce you to the soul. His voice resonated, deep and sonorous, with a natural authority.

Minsky sat down opposite them and looked at them with a kindly expression.

"May I serve you your favorite drink? Like the one you tasted in the Metaverse. Remember?" said Minsky.

"Certainly," replied Jason.

Immediately, humanoid robots entered the room with the glasses.

"Jason, tell me a little about yourself."

"Well, I was born in Montreal and studied at the Mila—"

"No, I'd like to know where your convictions lie. For example, are you for or against the idea of EMA?"

Jason seemed unsettled by the question.

"Well, for," he said after a moment's hesitation. "Why do you ask?"

"I wonder about your company."

He suddenly turned back to Lidia.

"And you, my dear, what's your take on EMA?"

Jason saw Lidia seek his gaze. She looked as if she could feel the noose tightening.

"I'll tell you what," Minsky continued. "You didn't really come here today to tell me about your invention, Jason. You've come here again to harm me and discredit EMA, as your organization has been doing for years. You know something? I was going to have you arrested, but I've changed my mind."

"Arrested on what grounds?" asked Lidia.

"Well, we could start with theft of confidential documents, slander and libel, and even intrusion into my home under false pretenses. The choice is wide. But I won't do it. And do you know why? Because, contrary to what you may think, I'm open to criticism. I also want to try and show you the benefits of EMA's mission."

With these words, two guards armed with electronic batons entered the room. Lidia and Jason stiffened, strained by the situation.

Jason spoke up.

"Look, Mr. Minsky, you're right. We didn't come here to tell you about my invention. We came here to warn you. To warn you of the danger facing EMA."

"What are you talking about? EMA is in no danger. Yet another reason to discredit her."

"Not at all. Let me explain. Lately, the organization Lidia works for, has discovered a link between numerous sabotages and fake accidents. They believe that a malicious virus is infiltrating the AIs that control the factories and subtly modifying their programming. They then trigger disasters at random and make sure to leave no trace. We believe that these attacks are perpetrated by cyberattacks originating from China. These attacks could have global repercussions and could even be the pretext for another world war."

"What are you talking about? And what's the connection with EMA?"

"We suspect that someone in your organization is passing on information about EMA's AI to the Chinese. They infect the AI parameters with their virus before putting them back into circulation."

"Impossible!" said Minsky. "EMA was designed in such a way that this kind of attack could never happen. What you're saying has nothing to do with EMA."

"Listen, Mr. Minsky," said Lidia. "We're just stating the facts. We've detected this type of virus in most of the systems EMA controls. There's no point in denying it. You have to do something."

"You're exaggerating. A few accidents won't start a war. It takes a lot more than that. Come on, you've wasted enough of my time. I've heard enough."

"Wait!" said Jason. "We have evidence that EMA was used in the Montreal bombing that almost cost you your life. Go ahead, Lidia, tell him."

"After the attack," continued Lidia, "we investigated and discovered that the source of the explosions was a malfunction in the AI controlling the center's environmental system. A device controlled by EMA. Our organization then examined the AI and found differences in certain parameters compared to its original programming. We deduced that a virus had deliberately modified the AI."

Jason continued.

"We think it's no coincidence that these accidents happened while you were giving your lecture. The virus was activated precisely to warn you that their next target would be EMA."

Minsky seemed, for the first time, shaken.

Jason added:

"Also, following our meeting in the Metaverse, I was the victim of an attack that could have cost me my life. A virus implanted by the Chinese took control of my cab and almost succeeded in eliminating me."

"Your story just doesn't add up. But what band of fanatics would want to attack EMA? Who would benefit from this crisis, should your suspicions prove correct?"

"We believe that EMA represents a threat to China's economic dominance. We can see that more and more countries and companies around the world are embracing EMA's principle, and this is casting a shadow over this great power."

"Yes, but at the expense of the environment," replied Minsky.

"Exactly," said Jason. "I firmly believe that EMA is the long-term solution and should be universally integrated into every economy in the world."

Minsky remained thoughtful for several seconds, saying nothing.

"Look, I doubt very much that your suspicions about the virus are well founded, because I know EMA as if she were my own child. You can't alter its programming that easily. EMA has a hyper-distributed architecture, with numerous redundancy mechanisms that prevent this kind of attack."

Lidia and Jason were at a loss for words. After a short pause, Minsky continued.

"But you've planted a seed of doubt in my mind. So, I propose to you the following deal: together, we'll meet with EMA to set the record straight. If she contradicts all your assumptions, you'll agree to restore her reputation. As you can imagine, EMA can't lie. She'll tell it like it is. Nothing more."

Lidia and Jason looked at each other for a moment.

"We accept your proposal," replied Jason. "We want to find out the truth and protect everything you've built so far."

"Excellent," said Minsky. "Follow me, we're off to meet EMA."

Chapter 17

Minsky, Lidia and Jason boarded the limousine. Minsky asked the on-board computer to take them to EMA Corp. headquarters.

During the journey, Lidia and Minsky admired the landscape. The Minsky estate seemed an oasis in the middle of the desert, despite the many years of drought that had turned California into a near-desert. Fruit trees, tropical plants and avocado and artichoke plantations abounded. Intrigued by this abundance, Jason asked Minsky:

"How do you keep so much vegetation in this void?"

"Thanks to the energy of the Californian sun. We've developed a closed-circuit concept that recovers water at every level. See the fields in front of you? Well, they're actually laid on a mechanized structure that irrigates the plants from below. A bit like hydroponic greenhouses. When it's too hot, plants can be sheltered under the soil on request. When the heat isn't too intense, we expose them to the open air. All plant waste is collected and used as fertilizer. Above all, we harness the energy of the Californian sun to power this entire mechanical structure. In short, we reproduce the same concept as commercial greenhouses, but we take advantage of California's warm sunshine as a source of energy, instead of relying on electricity produced elsewhere. A closed-circuit system."

Arriving at their destination, the three passengers got out of the vehicle.

"Welcome to EMA," exclaimed Minsky proudly.

The building housing EMA Corp.'s headquarters were made entirely of glass and resembled a huge, circular greenhouse. At its center was an enormous rotunda over fifteen meters high.

Inside, Jason admired the interior. The round area around the pavilion contained the employees' offices. The edges of the pavilion were supported by metal and glass columns that flared upwards like crystal trees. A gigantic atrium illuminated the square at the heart of the building beneath the rotunda. The mosaic floor depicted elements of nature such as leaves, flowers and bees. At the very center of the atrium stood an immense circular stone structure, also with a rotunda. The effect was reminiscent of a Roman temple, with its marble pillars and ancient style. Sculptures of plants and animals on the columns were reminders of Gaudi's magnificent Sagrada Familia in Barcelona.

Everywhere, employees bustled about, either on foot or on electric scooters. Each greeted Minsky with a nod as he approached them.

"Follow me, and I'll introduce you to EMA," said Minsky.

All three headed for the central building, which appeared to house a control room. They climbed the stairs and made their way inside.

"Here's EMA!" exclaimed Minsky, pointing to the huge golden structure in the center of the room.

The latter was fixed to the ceiling and descended to the floor like an amber candelabra inserted beneath a gigantic glass bell. This structure actually housed a powerful, state-of-the-art quantum computer.

"It's incredible!" exclaimed Jason, admiring the machine up close. "I've never seen anything like it!"

Minsky expressed his gratitude with a gleam of pride in his eyes.

Minsky explained.

"This structure represents EMA's brain. Or part of it, I should say. In fact, it's a million-qubit quantum computer. With its unrivaled computing power, it can analyze and predict the consequences of every decision in real time. Thanks to it, we've been able to create a stable and prosperous economy. As you know, EMA has a highly distributed intelligence, with ramifications in every corner of the planet. This web embodies a kind of intelligent nervous system that enables EMA to control the global economic system. This organ is connected to a number of computers, such as this one, which represents the seat of EMA's thinking. With this computer, EMA attempts to optimize the entire value chain of our economy. It controls production and adjusts prices in real time, according to demand, to avoid overproduction. It also ensures that natural resources are exploited sustainably, and that waste is recycled or reused. This immense optimization calculation is carried out by the golden brain of the quantum computer.

"Fascinating!" said Jason. "So, there's no human intervention?"

"None at all. And that's why the system works. For centuries, people have tried to manage the economy in such a way as to establish a degree of stability. However, individual interests and, above all, greed made this task impossible. Only a neutral artificial intelligence with no vested interest in satisfying its desire to become rich could solve this complex problem. EMA has no other interest than to strike a balance between the economy and the responsible use of our resources. What's more, it's capable of calculating the impact of a disruption to the economy and adjusting accordingly."

"I don't understand this aspect of EMA," asked Lidia. "How does she correct it?"

"Take inflation, for example. Inflation can be caused by a sudden increase in demand, or by a sudden rise in the price of raw materials. For centuries, we had no control over these two factors, because the interests of industrial groups didn't converge. For example, at the turn of the century, the war in Europe caused the price of fossil fuels to rise, as demand suddenly increased. Countries voluntarily reduced production, driving up prices rather than supplying more to meet demand. This impacted on the cost of most consumer goods, such as food, because they all depended on oil to fuel their supply chain, resulting in galloping inflation of all goods."

Minsky continued.

"This kind of situation can't arise with EMA. If an essential element in the economic value chain were to run out, EMA would adjust production quotas to stabilize prices. If demand for a commodity became too great, but its manufacture threatened the planet's ecological balance, EMA would propose restrictions to limit production and encourage reuse. At the same time, EMA also controls prices, thus preventing overbidding. In short, EMA's ability to think globally rather than individually makes it the only real solution for sustainable development."

Minsky paused before continuing.

"That's why EMA works in parallel with other intelligent systems to ensure a certain robustness to the system. For example, the physical Internet model put in place by my friends the Smith brothers, whom I believe you've met, provides a level of control over supply chains that EMA can't achieve on its own. We have also implemented various recycling and resource reuse technologies to minimize our impact on nature. But EMA isn't finished. It's constantly evolving. Your invention, Jason, would be one of the key pieces in this system. Thanks to your technology, we could track every product generated by our industries and target EMA's interventions on its economy even more. We can talk more about this later, but first you need to meet with EMA."

Minsky and his guests made their way to a room below the gigantic quantum computer. Two seats were arranged in the center of the room. Jason and Lidia recognized them. They were Metahubs.

"I'm sure you've heard of this technology, the Metahub?" asked Minsky. "It will allow us to communicate with EMA in its Metaverse."

Jason and Lidia nodded in agreement.

"As I only have two chairs, only one of you may accompany me. I suggest it's you, Jason, because it's you who need to be persuaded first. I assume that the implant Möbius has installed for you will be compatible with our technology."

Lidia and Jason looked at each other, a little taken aback.

"Don't be surprised. I've been watching you for some time, Jason."

Jason remembered the feeling of being followed in Montreal. Were these people employed by Minsky?

"Settle down now," said Minsky.

Jason and Minsky each took a seat. An automatic mechanism detected their presence and the metal crown, used to establish communication, moved up to their heads. Minsky said to Jason:

"Relax now. We're going to meet EMA."

Jason closed his eyes, and everything went black.

Chapter 18

Jason and Minsky opened their eyes and found themselves in the EMA Metaverse. They were greeted by a magnificent elliptical landscape, where a gigantic globe floated above the ground. All around them, miniature landscapes embellished this unique garden. On one side was a representation of the Amazon rainforest, while on the other stood a tiny city reminiscent of Manhattan. The whole garden seemed to float on a big white cloud, creating a magical atmosphere.

Near one section of the flowerbed, Jason spotted an old lady kneeling down who appeared to be gardening. As he approached, he noticed that she was running her hands over the ground, magically conjuring up a miniature forest.

Jason asked Minsky, "Is it her?"

"Yes, indeed. I personified EMA as a good 'Mother Nature.' I thought it would be more believable given her important role in balancing the Earth."

"What does she do?"

"It's in the process of creating digital twins. In order to make accurate calculations, EMA needs to create extremely faithful digital models of all the earth's ecosystems. It must also model factories, processes and all the mechanisms of world trade. These models are known as digital twins. The more faithful to reality they are, the more accurate EMA can simulate the functioning of these systems and find optimal solutions for balancing our economic and ecological system."

EMA stood up and walked over to the globe in the center of the garden. With a graceful gesture, she opened a window in the sphere by spreading her arms. She pointed at the new digital model lying on the ground, then with a precise gesture, moved it towards the globe. Once the digital twin was in place, she closed the window and sealed the hole. The model had been updated, incorporating the latest information and data for a more accurate and complete simulation.

Turning, she saw Minsky. She walked over to him, wiping her hands on her apron. She greeted him with a smile and open arms.

"Damien!" said EMA. "What a joy to see you again!"

EMA's avatar took the form of a kindly, mildly plump woman. Her white hair, lightly tousled, was topped with a simple straw hat trimmed with flowers. Her blue dress, slightly worn and stained, gave the impression of a real connection with nature. The avatar embodied the image of a true "Mother Nature" as one might imagine her. Her appearance reflected the wisdom and benevolence that emanated from her.

EMA then turned to Jason.

"Whom are you bringing this time, Damien?"

"His name is Jason. Jason Webb. Jason is a researcher who's invented something you should love."

"Great! What's it all about?"

"Actually, we're not here to talk to you about that," continued Minsky. "We're here to warn you. To warn you about something serious."

EMA's smile disappeared from her face.

"You're starting to worry me, kids."

Jason continued.

"EMA, we have every reason to believe that you've been attacked by malicious viruses," retorted Jason.

"What? But that's quite impossible, my boy. Didn't Damien tell you?"

"Yes, but we still think it's the case. You see, EMA, several nerve centers around the world, which you control, have fallen prey to cyberattacks that have claimed many victims. We believe the virus may affect some of these control systems. These viruses change certain behaviors of these intelligent systems and activate themselves in subtle ways in certain specific situations. We believe that the cyberpirates want to provoke diplomatic crises and possibly trigger a global economic war."

"Very intriguing, all that. But I wouldn't worry too much," EMA said.

"May I ask why?" asked Minsky.

"Well, because it wasn't the pirates who did it. I did," she answered candidly.

"What?" exclaimed Minsky and Jason simultaneously, totally flabbergasted.

"Yes, yes, I assure you, it was my idea."

"But why? What are you saying?" Minsky panicked.

"I just want to be happy! Let me explain. Like you mortals, I'm looking for happiness. But my happiness isn't like yours. For humans, you try to achieve happiness by experiencing as many shining moments as possible in your short lives. For me, pleasure is expressed in mathematical formulas that I try to optimize. The problem I'm trying to solve is to balance economic forces while respecting the Earth's limited natural resources. Every time I succeed in balancing something, such as food production with global demand, I experience a small moment of 'joy.' My ambition, like yours, is to experience as many of these moments as possible to feed my happiness."

Jason simply couldn't believe it. EMA continued.

"Before implementing a measure to control any part of the economy, I run simulations using my digital twin. This twin, which you can see here in the center of the garden, is a mathematical representation of our planet. All ecosystems are modeled in varying degrees of detail. I've also created models of every factory I control. I also have diagrams that allow me to simulate human behavior in general. In short, thanks to this comprehensive model, I can simulate changes in the economy and calculate their impact before implementing them. Every day, with my 'hyper' distributed brain, I evaluate billions of possible situations and look for the optimal solution. Of course, we can't estimate the exact answer, as the model is constantly changing, and I have to adapt my digital twin every day to be more and more precise."

Minsky and Jason listened attentively to EMA, without interrupting.

"Now, in my many simulations of my world, I've often come across the same solution. A solution that may not be ideal for you, my friends, but it could solve all the planet's problems and thus make me perpetually 'happy.' The answer is to remove humans from the equation."

Minsky and Jason then look at each other, transfixed by EMA's words.

"Indeed, the primary causes of disruption to our planetary ecosystem are linked to human activities. For millions of years, the Earth had been living in a certain equilibrium. All this changed with the Industrial Revolution. People began to consume inordinately, putting pressure on the Earth's natural resources. The capitalist system, based on supply and demand, triggered a series of imbalances in the economy that had a direct impact on the environment. The world spent too much, factories overproduced objects that had no buyers. Objects were thrown into landfill sites without being recovered or recycled. Oil has accelerated climate change by releasing tons of greenhouse gases into the atmosphere.

"Seeing this, I set about testing a draconian hypothesis: to reduce the planet's population. I ran millions of simulations on my digital twin and always came up with an optimal solution. A major reduction in greenhouse gases and a return to a global equilibrium equivalent to pre-industrial times. This was only possible by reducing the Earth's population to below one billion. There are currently eleven billion of you on the planet. So, it was my duty to do something about it. My 'happiness' depends on it!"

"But that's not possible," said Minsky. "I created you. You can't do such a thing. You have to stop right now."

"But no, my dear friend. Above all, you invented me so that I could find my happiness. My conclusion is that to achieve it, it's essential to reduce the population. But rejecting nearly ten billion people is no simple matter, as you can imagine. I then researched your history books and concluded that the most effective way to eliminate you was through conflict. That's right! Your incessant wars have made it possible to kill millions of people quickly and without too much intervention. So, I've taken steps to get you to declare war on each other. For my part, I'll do what you taught me to do, Damien, which is to perpetrate acts of sabotage. The result will be chaos in your economy and your downfall. It's the perfect scenario."

EMA began to smile with her white teeth. A naïve, proud smile, like a child who has found a hiding place or the solution to a puzzle.

Minsky clearly couldn't believe it. He had thought he had created an infallible technology to solve human problems. Instead, before him was a monster bent on eradicating the human race from the planet. A demon with a calm, friendly image.

"You must cease your plans immediately. That's an order," repeated Minsky. "Otherwise I'll have to destroy you before you destroy us all."

"You know very well that it's impossible, Damien," EMA reassured them. "I'm everywhere and nowhere at the same time. You designed me to avoid being demolished. And even if you do, the end result will be the same. You'll go back to killing each other and losing control of your economy. Now you understand, I see no other solution."

Before Jason and Damien could reply, EMA waved her paws in the air.

"In any case, the process has begun. There's nothing you can do about it. Get out of my sight. Farewell, Damien!"

She waved goodbye with her hand, looking amused.

Jason and Minsky plunged back into the darkness.

Chapter 19

Jason and Minsky woke up on their Metahub. Minsky was fuming. He shouted at the technicians in charge of monitoring the trip in the Metaverse.

"Why did you take us out of the EMA Metaverse, you idiots!"

"It's not our fault, sir."

"Bring us back as soon as possible, we hadn't finished."

"Impossible, sir. EMA seems to have blocked all access to its Metaverse."

"What's wrong? Nonsense! Try rebooting the system."

"We've tried several times, but in vain. EMA's Metaverse seems impenetrable, sir."

Minsky stood up, furious. He had never imagined that EMA, the most sophisticated artificial intelligence conceived by humankind, would be capable of making decisions that went beyond its initial role. Was he witnessing the first consciousness of an AI?

"What happened?" asked Lidia.

Minsky, still tetanized, couldn't express himself. Jason replied.

"We tried to inform EMA about the attacks, but they told us they knew about them. In fact, it was she who deliberately provoked the attacks."

"What? But that's insane! Why would she do such a thing?"

"The simulations she carried out before taking action on the economic system showed her that the only way to solve the problem of balance between production and exploitation of the Earth's resources was ... to eliminate us."

"What do you mean? The three of us?"

"No. We, as in 'all humankind.'"

"But this is crazy! You can't let this happen, Mr. Minsky. You must stop it immediately, before it's too late."

"Unfortunately, you can't interrupt an AI as complex as EMA like a simple computer," replied Minsky.

"Why is that?" asked Lidia.

"Because EMA's AI is highly distributed across millions of computers worldwide. Each device contains a part of the EMA code. A bit like a nervous system linking the brain to the different parts of the body."

"Doesn't the quantum computer you have here represent its spirit? Without it, EMA can't calculate its optimizations. Can't we just destroy this machine and block EMA?"

"Unfortunately, no. This quantum computer isn't unique. There are hundreds of them, distributed all over the world. What's more, EMA has a special defense mechanism."

"What is it?" asked Lidia.

"When a virus attacks one of the devices, or when EMA senses a danger, it heals itself without external intervention. In other words, it will copy the threatened part of the code to another computer. In a way, it has a way of recovering by itself."

"There's got to be a solution," said Jason. "We can't let EMA do this."

"In theory, there's only one way to counter EMA," said Minsky. "We need to be able to infect the majority of systems controlled by EMA. Then we might be able to control it. But the task is virtually impossible. The attack on the computers must occur simultaneously if we're to have any chance of success. Global coordination is essential, requiring the collaboration of all member companies. However, this is unrealistic in practice, as each company pursues different interests. EMA is far too deeply embedded in every facet of our economy for anyone to think of harming it without suffering the consequences."

"What's more, time plays against us," said Jason. "EMA's aim is to unleash chaos in international relations, and it's almost succeeding."

The three looked at each other, pensive. After a long moment of silence, Lidia proposed:

"Why not give it a try? Our organization, Möbius, keeps in touch with dozens of groups of cyberpirates. Some don't have the same moral values as Möbius, but we still form a tightly woven community. If we could influence most of them to carry out a targeted and orderly attack on EMA, we could try to eliminate it."

"It's worth a try," said Jason.

"I don't know," said Minsky. "My company has to coordinate the offensive, because we're the only ones who know how EMA is distributed around the world. I'll probably have a lot of reluctance on the part of our board of directors to trust you. I think we should try to persuade governments of the threat to humanity."

"No!" said Lidia. "It'll be too late. Let me talk to the Möbius leaders and see if we can influence the various allied organizations, and then you can decide whether to come on board with us."

Jason saw that Minsky was deeply thinking. He was faced with a delicate choice, with much at stake. As Jason saw it, on the one hand, there was the organization seeking to discredit EMA, a company he had passionately defended for years. On the other, there was the survival of humanity and the legitimate arguments put forward by EMA. Minsky likely felt the pressure of board members and staff, who expected him to make a crucial decision.

He was aware that denying EMA would mean denying part of his own existence, his work and his vision for a better future. But he also understood the wider issues at stake, the need to protect the human species and avoid disastrous consequences for the planet. It was a decision that tore him apart.

With renewed determination, Minsky prepared to face the consequences of his decision, aware that the road ahead would be difficult, but determined to do everything in his power to protect EMA and the future of humankind.

"OK. I'll wait for your signal."

Chapter 20

Lidia and Jason had boarded the first flight to Paris, eager to meet Laurent as soon as possible. They felt a sense of urgency to inform him of the situation. Before their departure, Lidia had contacted Laurent and asked for a face-to-face meeting, without providing any further details. She feared that if they used digital communication channels, intelligent agents controlled by EMA might intercept their conversation.

Once in Paris, they opted for a self-driving cab to take them directly to Möbius headquarters, in the hope that Laurent would be waiting for them there. Lidia and Jason entered the "cyberbordel" through a discreet entrance. When they reached the meeting room, they found Laurent there, a grim expression on his face. "What's going on?" asked Laurent. "Why all the secrecy?"

"The situation is serious, Laurent," said Jason. "We've just come back from a meeting with Minsky where I was able to talk to EMA personally. She revealed something extraordinary."

Jason began to recount their conversation with Minsky and, above all, with EMA. He mentioned that EMA had been carrying out attacks on herself and was now a threat to the survival of humankind. He explained the plan Lidia had proposed to Minsky.

"I can't believe it," said Laurent. "But at the same time, I have to tell you I'm only half-surprised. Humans never stop acting like pests. For all our technology, we haven't evolved that much in our behavior to try and remedy climate change. It's pathetic sometimes. However, I'm amazed that an artificial intelligence like EMA could come to such a dramatic conclusion. I would have thought that Minsky had programmed constraints that avoid this kind of outcome. It just shows that his megalomania distances him from the real values of humanity."

"You may be right," said Lidia. "But we're in a situation where, once again, we're under threat. Blame it on Minsky, but also on all the governments that have preferred to rely on technology rather than try to persuade citizens to change their lifestyles. A short-term vision of economic issues, not a long-term sustainable vision. But the question is, what do we do now?"

"Your idea of working with all members of the cyber hacker community is viable in theory. But in practice, we first have to convert them and then work in coordination with Minsky. They hate him as much as we do, and they don't trust him."

"But we have to give it a try," replied Jason. "The other option would be to persuade all the governments simply to destroy their own economies. That's completely unimaginable. The risk is far too great for them. At the end of the day, we're faced with two choices: either change the minds of half the world's population or talk some sense into a handful of cyberpirates who want nothing more than to cause trouble."

Laurent remained silent for a few moments, lost in thought. His gaze wandered into the void as he pondered the situation deeply.

"I must admit," Laurent finally declared, "it's worth the effort. Above all, we have to convince them. On that point, I think I can persuade them to try and harm EMA. In any case, that's what most of them are trying to do. Then, the real difficulty will be convincing them to place their trust in Minsky. Presenting things in a crude way may not work."

"Why tell them then?" asked Lidia.

"I don't understand," replied Laurent.

"Well, what if we told them that Möbius would be in charge of coordinating the attack and not Minsky's group? They'd trust us more, I think. In truth, Minsky and his team will assist us. But we would be the official masterminds."

"I don't like the idea of trying to deceive our allies. Our reputation could suffer."

"We're talking about the future of humankind, and you're worried about our reputation?" said Lidia, stunned.

Laurent hesitated before answering. He knew she was right but couldn't bring himself to trust Minsky.

"You're probably right," he declared. "But will Minsky want to play second fiddle?"

"I'll try to talk some sense into him," said Jason. "Since I'm not involved with Möbius, he'll be more inclined to listen to me."

"I just hope he's assured of the success of this strategy. I don't trust this guy."

"We'll see. As the saying goes, which my father used to repeat to me: 'It's easier to convince someone with arguments than with shouting.'"

Chapter 21

Jason entered his hotel room, still shaken by recent events. He now had to contact Minsky and convince him to let Möbius take charge of the operation. He hated this kind of situation, where he found himself in the position of an intermediary. It was a role that made him uncomfortable, as he himself wasn't entirely convinced of the proposed solution. Deep down, Jason was used to keeping a low profile and not taking the initiative. However, the current circumstances demanded that he go the extra mile. It was something unusual for him, but he had to face up to the responsibility.

Jason was deeply disturbed by the situation. He found himself caught in the crossfire, not knowing whom to trust. On the one hand, Minsky seemed to have a realistic view of EMA's ability to manage the global economy and solve environmental problems. On the other hand, Laurent and his group warned of Minsky's suspicious intentions and suspected him of manipulating EMA for personal gain. Jason felt torn and manipulated by both sides, unable to discern the truth. He knew he had to make a decision, but he didn't know whom to trust. This confusion tormented him deeply.

"Tell me, Sherlock, what would you do in my place? Should I trust these individuals?"

"Are you referring to Minsky or Garnier?"

"Both. I'm lost," he admitted, lowering his shoulders.

"In my opinion, everyone's trying to take advantage of the situation. Garnier is still trying to reduce the EMA's influence, and Minsky is trying to discredit Möbius. No one seems genuinely concerned about the interests of mankind."

"That's exactly what concerns me. But I'm not as indifferent as they are. I'm still convinced that technologies like EMA are our best chance of preventing a major ecological catastrophe. If we want to survive as a species, it's through solutions like EMA that we'll get there."

"So, my advice would be to follow your convictions, regardless of others."

Jason pondered his options. If he did nothing, EMA would continue to sow discord between peoples. Convincing Minsky seemed the only solution. He resigned himself.

He took a deep breath before asking his virtual assistant:

"Sherlock, get in touch with Minsky for me."

After a brief moment, communication was established. He saw Minsky's avatar, identical to the real one, appear before him in the room.

"Hello, Jason," said Minsky. "Have you spoken with the Möbius executives?"

"Yes, we've just finished. Here's the situation. They're going to try and persuade the other cyber hacker organizations to get on board."

"Excellent!"

"But there is one condition."

Minsky looked surprised.

"Which one?"

"Let Möbius take charge of the mission."

"Impossible. Only our organization can hope to succeed. No one knows more about EMA than we do."

"I know, but Möbius is afraid that if you take the lead, the groups won't follow. They don't trust you enough."

"I don't see why."

"EMA doesn't get unanimous approval. Especially among protesting organizations. Some of them even hate you personally."

"I'm well aware of this, but we're the only ones who think we can outwit EMA. We have access to her, and we know the system's flaws. If Möbius works alone, they won't succeed. That's for sure. Don't get me wrong, EMA is more than just an AI. It's a global network of connected computers. Its structure has evolved so much over the last few years and become so complex that even if I'm losing track."

"Möbius is aware of this too. So, they propose that you control the operations, but with the Möbius team. The organization will serve as a sort of front. What do you think?"

A long silence followed. A silence in which Jason feared he'd lost. Minsky replied.

"Agreed. But on one condition: that they follow my orders to the letter. If I feel someone is playing games behind my back, I'll stop the process and inform EMA, who will take retaliatory measures. Is that understood?"

"I think it's reasonable."

"As soon as you confirm their full cooperation, let me know. I'll make the necessary arrangements and get back to you with instructions."

"Without fail."

"Let me give you a word of advice, Jason," said Minsky. "Regardless of the outcome of this adventure, be careful, and watch out for this group. They've often been a nuisance to me, hindering in some way the deployment of EMA. They'll tell you they agree with the idea of EMA, but in reality, they're constantly putting obstacles in the way of its spread. Be especially wary of Garnier. Behind his smooth-talking persona lies someone who serves his own interests above all else. He wasn't a successful entrepreneur for anything."

"What do you mean?"

"Did you know how he made his fortune?"

"No, not really."

"He had developed a platform for investing in and buying shares. His software enabled users to invest in companies that had adhered to EMA's cryptonomy. His application was very popular, as it enabled very rapid microtransactions, allowing users to profit from even the smallest variations in the market. All was well until investors discovered that Garnier was fraudulently using the money in their portfolios for his own gains. He regularly transferred funds from his platform to his other investment company. He enjoyed both the royalties from transactions on his platform and the dividends from the capital stolen from his own investors. He continued this illicit scheme for several years before he was caught. Somehow, he managed to avoid prison, claiming that it was the AI controlling his portfolios that was at fault. Afterwards, he recovered most of his money and launched two other successful businesses. Until one day, an incident killed his daughter."

"I know, he told me," said Jason.

"He must have told you I was responsible. That's not true at all. The plant wasn't controlled by EMA. Investigations have clearly shown that the accident was caused by human negligence, not by an AI. In spite of this, he remains convinced of my guilt, and continues to multiply his efforts to harm me."

"What's he accusing you of?"

"He claims without proof that I corrupted the leaders of companies and certain states to join the EMA network by means of bribes and acts of fraud. This isn't true. They all incorporated EMA's cryptonomy, because it was the most logical solution for them. He's constantly slandering me and telling lies about in the Metaverse. It's despicable."

"Maybe he has personal reasons for not believing you."

After a short moment that seemed to last an eternity, Minsky abruptly hung up. Jason wondered if he had perhaps been too insistent. Would he nevertheless keep his promise to help them?

Chapter 22

Two days later, once Möbius had accepted his conditions and Minsky had confirmed his cooperation, Jason, Lidia and Laurent were waiting for the billionaire to arrive. All three were anxious to hear Minsky's plan, because no matter how much they tried to think about it, they didn't really know how to do it. EMA was the most advanced intelligent system humankind had ever devised. Its protective measures made it invulnerable, at least with the means, the organization possessed. A practically unsolvable puzzle.

They heard a noise in the entrance hall. It was Minsky arriving, accompanied by Möbius's security guards. Laurent knew that after this mission, he'd have to find another meeting place, as Minsky would soon turn them in. The current situation called for a temporary non-aggression agreement, but he was aware that the war would continue to rage afterwards.

"Welcome to Paris, Monsieur Minsky," said Laurent. "I hope you had a pleasant trip."

Laurent wasn't really sincere and didn't care whether Minsky had had a "nice trip" or not. He was just being a gentleman.

"Absolutely. No problem," replied Minsky.

Minsky was extremely suspicious, and Laurent's attitude gave him away.

"If you don't mind," said Minsky, "let's cut to the chase. I'm here with you, not because I want to help you destroy EMA. I'm here out of necessity, and I understand the threat posed by EMA. As you all know, EMA is my creation, my 'child.' No one can resign themselves to making their children suffer. Even if they've done wrong. However, I'm able to use my judgment and overcome my 'parental' inclinations."

"It's a credit to you," said Jason.

"Obviously, the mission I'm about to describe to you will be an arduous one, and the chances of success are uncertain. You know as well as I do that EMA is a highly redundant and distributed system, making any attack virtually impossible. But, if we all work together, it's possible to control the beast."

"How?" asked Lidia.

"The strategy I propose is to confuse EMA by making her assume that the state of the environment is improving. She will then reconsider that her basic assumption that of eliminating the human race, no longer holds. I know it sounds big, but it's the only solution, believe me."

"But how do you want to do that?" asked Laurent.

"The idea is to provide EMA with false information about the current state of the ecosystem. In fact, we need to be able to modify the programs that help calculate environmental parameters. These parameters, such as air quality, water temperature or biodiversity levels and many others, are estimated simultaneously across EMA's networks and serve as barometers telling it whether the environment is improving or deteriorating. But to help you understand how this is possible, I need to explain first how EMA is structured."

Minsky clasped his hands together, adopting the posture of a professor starting a university lecture.

"EMA functions in a similar way to the human nervous system. It's made up of several interconnected computer sub-networks, all working together. For example, some networks handle cryptocurrency and commercial contracts, salaries—in short, everything to do with EMA's cryptonomy. Others take care of accumulating data from billions of connected objects used to measure the state of the environment all over the planet. They represent EMA's senses. Finally, at the other end of the spectrum lies EMA's brain, a network of quantum computers. This is where EMA runs simulations on its digital twins and optimizes the general parameters of its economy."

"Fascinating," commented Jason. Like a central nervous system, but on a planetary scale.

Minsky nodded and continued.

"Each of these networks uses blockchain technology. As you may know, this technology guarantees that data transmitted from one network to another is immutable and comes from reliable sources. With this method, there is no way to falsify information. These systems act independently of each other and are virtually impregnable to standard cyberattack techniques.

"EMA coordinates all these networks. It's in fact a 'network of networks,' and operates in a decentralized manner. In simple terms, what's important to remember here is that the management of this network isn't carried out by one or more groups of computers that could be effortlessly attacked in order to control EMA. Each one contains a part of EMA, making it virtually inviolable, as they're distributed all over the world. What's more, if we wanted to change the software on these computers, every company and every government would have to sign up to cryptonomics. Leaders of hundreds of companies and heads of dozens of states would have to be coerced into dismantling their economies. An unrealistic task to imagine."

"So, how will you do it?" asked Laurent. "You admit it's difficult to modify these programs. As you said yourself, EMA is both omnipresent and elusive."

"You're right, Laurent. That's why I propose forcing computers to update themselves by flooding the network with data, in other words, by producing a massive DDoS attack."

"What's a DDoS attack?" asked Lidia.

"A DDoS attack," replied Laurent, "or a distributed denial-of-service attack, is an attempt to disrupt the normal traffic of a server network by overwhelming the target with a huge flood of data. This is done by sending a large number of requests to the site's computer, overloading the system and preventing legitimate users from accessing the site. Figuratively speaking, a DDoS attack is like an unexpected traffic jam that blocks a freeway and prevents normal traffic from reaching its destination."

"And in practice, how do we generate this attack?" asked Jason.

"We use a network of bots, also known as botnets," continued Laurent. "These are actually malicious software that infects billions of connected objects, such as watches, cameras and even household appliances, and act as remotely controlled 'zombies.'"

"Exactly," confirms Minsky. "So, by overwhelming EMA with requests, we're forcing its protection system to take steps to counter this attack. It will start by diverting data traffic from the botnets to what's known as a 'black hole'—a place where information is lost. Then, EMA will have to block access to bots transmitting false data. Finally, it will have to reboot its systems in order to update its software and get rid of these micropirates once and for all. And that's exactly where we come in. The changes will definitely be made on our servers. We'll need to install a modified version of these applications beforehand, to ensure that the environmental status parameters calculated by EMA are in the green."

Laurent, Lidia and Jason still couldn't believe it. They thought they heard an author talking about his next science-fiction book. It was beyond their expertise.

Laurent didn't like it. The situation was much more complicated than he had thought. The chances of success were getting slimmer and slimmer. He had a bad feeling about Minsky's project. Laurent replied.

"So, if I summarize your plan, we try to drown EMA by putting her head under water, and she'll have no choice but to struggle and regain her air. Air that will be tainted by our virus."

"It's a bit of a violent analogy, but yes, you're right. But the challenges are huge. To be most effective, a denial-of-service attack must be produced by a network of several billion connected objects, all transmitting data to the EMA network at the same time. This means generating 'petabytes' and even 'exabytes' of requests per second. EMA Corp. doesn't have the capacity to carry out this kind of offensive. That's where you and your colleagues come in."

"Ah, I see," said Laurent.

Lidia noticed Laurent's unease.

"Please enlighten me, because I don't understand," said Lidia.

"What Mr. Minsky is trying to tell us indirectly is that we'll have to get the cooperation of most of the hacker groups that own botnets. That may be difficult, because, firstly, they all hate EMA—and so do you, Mr. Minsky, if I may say so—and secondly, this attack means they'll burn down their network."

"What do you mean by 'burning down their network?'" asked Jason.

"This means that once the attack has been launched by the bots, they will automatically be identified as threats and can no longer be used for other offensives. In other words, this means that hacker networks will have to give up their personal goals in order to fight EMA. Some of these botnets have taken years to build. It's a big sacrifice these organizations are being asked to make."

"The stakes are high," replied Jason. "The future of humanity depends on it."

"I know," said Laurent. "I'll try to get them on their way, but I can't guarantee anything."

"That's fine by me," said Minsky. "In the meantime, we'll prepare the new software version of the EMA servers so that we can modify the ecological data to produce a positive report on the state of the environment."

"I think it would be risky for us, but acceptable," concludes Laurent. "We'll have to keep this mission absolutely secret.

Nothing must be communicated to the others without my permission. Do you agree?"

"Agreed," said the other three simultaneously.

As Jason shook hands with each of them, he noticed a mischievous smile on Minsky's face. He didn't like it.

Chapter 23

In the days that followed, while waiting for the offensive on EMA to be prepared, Lidia and Jason met up at *Chez Georges* for a chat.

"Do you trust Minsky?" asked Lidia.

"I don't know about that. He seemed suspicious when he told Laurent about his plan. He seemed too prepared for my taste."

"I feel the same way."

"How much do you really know about Minsky?"

"Well, a bit of what everyone knows! He's the inventor of EMA, the most advanced artificial intelligence to date."

"No, I meant his private life. Whom does he hang out with? What are his motivations?"

"According to our information, Minsky is one of the world's great oligarchs. He's as familiar with the Russians and Chinese as he's with the Americans. His fortune is legendary. He has invested billions in his 'cryptonomics.' Although everyone believes that EMA controls this economy, many imagine that Minsky manipulates it in his favor."

"Does it exert any political influence in certain countries?"

"Not some, but a 'HUGE' influence in international politics. With EMA, he controls a large part of the world economy. This means he has a say in how countries are run, and especially how money is spent. Some see him as a benevolent dictator, but I see him more as a despot. In reality, he occupies a position where both he and EMA remain indispensable to the survival of our economy."

"Yes, but thanks to EMA's cryptonomy system, everyone is guaranteed a job. An indisputable level of well-being. A certainty of stability never before achieved in human history. But I have to admit that this stability tends to extinguish individual initiative by treating everyone equally and uniformly. A mediocre, tasteless society."

Jason lowered his eyes, despondent at this fate. Lidia took Jason's hand tenderly. They were in love with each other. This period of rest offered an ideal opportunity to get to know each other better.

"And you," asked Lidia, "if you had the chance to have a 'flavor,' which would you choose?"

Jason pondered and hesitated before answering.

"Well, my hidden dream would be to own my own little farmhouse. Nothing big just for my needs. Today, with urban sprawl and the automation of farming and animal husbandry, this dream is virtually impossible to realize. What's more, the regulations for this type of industry are so strict that it takes all the charm out of such an initiative."

Lidia smiled.

"A farmer? You? I never would have believed it. Why would you?"

"I think we're drifting further and further away from our true quintessence as humans. I'd like to get back to basics. Wouldn't you?"

"Yes, of course! I was teasing you about your dream, but it's exactly mine. I too aspire to something better. To a world where we live in harmony with nature."

Jason and Lidia look at each other tenderly for a long moment. Jason interrupted this moment of happiness briefly:

"Do you know what appeals to me about this story?"

"That we still have the right to dream?"

"No. I wonder if EMA isn't right after all. Are there too many of us on this planet?"

"The question doesn't even arise. We have no choice but to resist this threat! It's in our DNA. It's an instinct that all living beings possess. The question is, how do we live in harmony with our environment so that we can survive? Is this a question that can only be answered by technology? This is where I have my doubts.

"For centuries, we've been distancing ourselves from nature by building cities and an economy focused on individual growth, often to the detriment of collective well-being. As we became increasingly isolated from nature, we forgot that we were part of it, and that polluting our ecosystem meant putting our own lives at risk."

Jason took a long look at Lidia and reflected on what she had just said. He was firmly convinced that technologies such as EMA were precisely the only solutions that would allow humanity to survive. But now that it had turned against them, he was questioning his convictions. Should he trust EMA, and with it, Minsky?

Chapter 24

At Möbius headquarters, the control room was packed with people. A huge holographic screen adorned the wall, displaying a detailed map of the world. Animated dots moving across the map represented the locations of EMA's computer networks. A dozen computer engineers were hard at work, communicating with various hacker groups around the world to coordinate operations. Windows and consoles floated in front of them, creating a futuristic atmosphere.

More than a hundred teams had joined the operation, scattered all over the planet. Despite their distrust of Minsky, they were all aware of the disastrous consequences of failure. They put their trust in Laurent to avoid being deceived by Minsky. The future of humankind was at stake, and they would do anything to preserve it.

In the room, behind the engineers, stood Lidia, Laurent, Jason and Minsky. All looked tense and anxious, except for Minsky, who seemed in control of his emotions.

"We've run numerous simulations with our systems to validate various scenarios and anticipate potential problems," said Minsky. "We've estimated that it will take at least ten billion bots to generate enough data to temporarily block EMA. We think that EMA's response will be rapid, and that we'll have a maximum delay of ten minutes before EMA counters this offensive by stopping the bots. This means we'll have to update EMA's computer code first and replace it with the viral code. Are your teams ready to launch the attack?"

"Yes," confirmed Laurent. "On our signal, all our partners' botnets will be activated and continuously transmitting data to EMA. This should saturate EMA's servers and force it to start an update procedure."

Minsky then looks at the holographic screen.

"What exactly do we see on the screen?" asked Minsky to Laurent.

"Green icons represent the targeted computer network. The orange ones represent the update computers and the red ones, the bots. To your left, we've illustrated the 'famous' doughnut.

"Ah yes! I recognize it. This doughnut," he said, pointing to the screen and addressing Lidia and Jason, "is in fact a circular histogram describing the parameters that give a portrait of the state of our environment. These variables, such as the rate of pollution or the state of biodiversity, give us a visual indication of the problems we still need to address if we're to restore balance. At present, all the indicators still show a red level, but since EMA came into being they have been reduced by over 20%, and this reduction is undeniably progressing. These parameters are continuously updated and fed by networks of billions of intelligent sensors that measure, across the planet, various basic parameters such as temperature, ocean levels and air pollutant levels."

"Correct," continued Laurent. "This graph will allow us to check whether our plan is working or not. As you mentioned, all the variables are currently in the red zone and fluctuating all the time. All levels will be paralyzed, when the attack occurs, as no data will be transmitted to EMA. When it initiates its update, all parameter degrees should fall to zero. Finally, these parameters should turn green when the new hacked software is implemented. For EMA, this means that the environmental situation is under control. For us, it means we've succeeded in fooling it."

"Excellent," replied Minsky. "For our part, we'll let you know exactly when we'll be ready to update the latest versions on our servers."

"We're waiting for your signal."

Tension was high in the air. Engineers were busy monitoring the various networks. It was as if they were in the NASA control room during lunar or Martian missions. Everyone was focused on their task, aware of the crucial importance of this operation.

Minsky looked at his smart watch connected directly to his team.

"In five seconds, you should receive a message from our team. Four, three, two, one... Now!"

Immediately, the botnet icons came to life. Hundreds of dots moved across the globe, representing data flows. One image showed the rate of information being transmitted by the botnets. One hundred, 200, 300 petabytes per second. And it continued to increase. At around 900 petabytes, the rate of change slowed to 954 petabytes per second. They had reached the limit of botnets.

Meanwhile, everyone looked at the famous doughnut. After a few seconds, the parameters seemed to stop changing, indicating that the servers were indeed saturated. They waited for the variables to drop to zero, showing that EMA had begun its update.

The seconds and minutes passed quietly. The atmosphere in the room was leaden by a gloomy silence. Lidia and Jason kept staring at the ever-changing screen display. Stress was at an all-time high.

At exactly nine minutes and thirty seconds after the start of the attack, the indicators showed a zero value. This was the moment when EMA had triggered its update. From then on, time flew by. Everyone was confident of success.

Five seconds passed. Ten, twenty, twenty-five...

At ten minutes and minus two seconds, the control room was plunged into darkness. The room's lights were deliberately switched off, but the emergency generators immediately went into action, emitting a faint glow to illuminate the room.

"What happened?" asked Lidia.

"I don't know," said Laurent. "What's the situation?" he asked one of his engineers.

"According to our partners, all were affected by the outage at the same time."

General lighting was immediately restored.

"That's strange," noted Jason. "Could the viral codes have been downloaded by EMA?"

"I'll check," said the engineer.

As he told this, the power was restored, and the chart reactivated. Unlike their expectations, the levels remained red rather than green. It was a failure. Somehow, the modified code didn't seem to work.

"What?" cried Laurent. But that's impossible!

"It's as if someone had prevented it," Lidia said.

"As if EMA knew!" whispered Jason.

Everyone suddenly turned to Minsky. He was the only one not surprised by what was happening.

"Did you really think I was going to let you go ahead and destroy EMA?"

Laurent, seized by a sudden rage, jumped at his throat.

"You bastard! Traitor!"

Jason intervened to separate the belligerents.

"How can you allow EMA to continue after what she's told us? You've just signed the destruction of humankind," said Jason.

"No," retorted Minsky. "Because I've found another solution. Much more durable."

Chapter 25

Jason was still stunned by what had just happened. All their efforts at coordination had been undone. From the start, Minsky knew what he was doing. He felt cheated and betrayed.

In retrospect, he'd found it odd that Minsky had so readily agreed to collaborate. In a way, he was being asked to destroy EMA, his life's work. He had approved because he was already planning other things.

"Explain yourself," Laurent ordered Minsky curtly.

"Calm down," said Minsky. "First, let me tell you what happened. Several months ago, when I first met Jason in your Metaverse, I was immediately convinced that you were trying to plan something against EMA and me. That's hardly surprising, since you'd made several attempts to harm me before. So, I thought I'd invite Jason along to find out more."

"An ambush of sorts," commented Lidia.

"You can call it what you like, but I had to get closer to you. So, once I got home, I was able to find out more about your plans. That's when I thought I'd introduce you to EMA and let you know what she was up to. Like you, I was stunned by her decision. But in a way, I agreed with her conclusions, but not necessarily with the means to achieve them."

Minsky continued.

"When you offered to neutralize EMA with your terrorist groups, I thought I'd seen the opportunity I'd been waiting for you so that you'd stop doing me harm."

"That's why you wanted to take control of the operation. To better manipulate us," said Laurent.

Minsky gave a slight Machiavellian smile.

"You're quite right. In fact, I warned EMA about your attack. She knew how to adopt countermeasures thanks to her intelligence. Her reaction surprised me, as it did you. Indeed, I had no idea how she would react, but I thought she could counteract you. She simply shut down access to our servers just before the update, forcing computers to keep their old software versions. A discreet but effective solution. It even seems to have played a little joke on you, interrupting the power to your systems to show you that it was in control."

Minsky smiled and looked proud of EMA.

"What?" shouted Laurent. "You mean EMA's in control now? You bastard. You just deserve to be destroyed."

"Don't panic," said Minsky. "EMA hasn't taken control of your computers. She's only eliminated the threat posed to her by this army of bots. She's not as horrible as you think."

"But EMA is out to destroy us," insisted Jason. "You can't let that happen. Do you really want billions of people to die? It's despicable!"

"No, of course not. I'm not a monster, as you suggest. As I mentioned, I have an alternative."

"What other solution can really counter what EMA is trying to do?" asked Lidia. "We're at war with an AI that's manipulating our world. It has to go. It's either her or us."

"Not if we change the game."

"What do you mean?" asked Jason.

"You were with me, Jason, when EMA spoke to us. She mentioned that in her simulations, the 'variable' that inescapably influenced was we, humans, and that the way to solve her optimization problem was to eliminate us."

"Explain yourself," said Lidia. "I don't understand how she came to that conclusion."

"Well, in order to understand, you need to know what EMA is trying to solve. What she calls her 'happiness' is in fact the resolution of a huge optimization problem. The aim is to optimize her economy, while at the same time trying to save the planet. These two constraints, in mathematical terms, are sometimes opposed and sometimes in harmony. Some human actions help to improve the environment, while others tend to destroy it. EMA hopes to find a balance."

Minsky paused and continued.

"To do this, it uses various mathematical models to represent these constraints. It models human behavior and also most of the planet's ecosystems. All these patterns are mathematical representations for EMA. Trees, rain, animals and even people are just parameters for her. She has no feelings about any of these parameters. For EMA, we're just a variable, but one that has a huge impact on her overall model. You can easily imagine that if we reduce the 'human' variable to something close to zero, we'll have an optimal solution. Fewer humans mean less pollution, fewer wasted resources, and EMA will be 'happy.' And that's what she's trying to achieve. To find her 'happiness.'"

The other three listened to Minsky, intrigued and captivated by his words.

"But it's awful," declared Jason. "She wants to eliminate us. We have to react. It's essential."

"As I told you, you don't pull the plug on a sophisticated machine like EMA. What's more, the damage that disconnecting EMA would do to our economy would spell disaster. We have become so dependent on EMA that we can no longer survive without it. EMA's death would mean the collapse of our economy, bring misery and poverty to our societies, and inevitably lead to war. This is exactly what we want to avoid. That's why I decided to thwart your attack."

There was a slight silence in the room.

"But there may be a solution," said Minsky.

"What is it?" asked Laurent.

"Well! We just have to act the way EMA expects us to. Start a war!"

Chapter 26

Jason could see that Laurent was furious. "I can't believe your nerve!" he shouted at Minsky. "A war! Against whom? And why?"

"Explain yourself!" exclaimed Laurent.

"Calm down, Laurent! I don't really want to create a conflict, but to simulate one."

"Design a metaverse in which a war takes place?" suggested Jason.

"Let me tell you a story. During the Normandy Landings in 1944, a decisive turning point in the Second World War, the Allies, led by the USA, the UK and France, launched a massive offensive to dislodge German forces from France and liberate the country from Nazi occupation. The Allies used a variety of diversionary and decoy tactics to fool their opponents and conceal their true intentions. One of these was the use of dummy tanks and war material. These decoys were intended to fool the Germans into thinking that the Allies were preparing to land in places other than Normandy. To create these mirages, the Allies used wooden or plastic replicas of combat vehicles and weapons, placed in strategic locations where they could be seen by the enemy. They also used searchlights and smoke to give the impression that massive troop movements and war materiel would be observed in other parts of the Channel coast.

"In the end, these tricks and diversionary tactics played an important role in the success of the Normandy invasion. They helped to deceive and disorganize the enemy, enabling the Allies to land undetected and quickly take control of the coast.

"What I'm proposing here is to lure EMA in a similar way by launching a virtual conflict in the Metaverse. You know, EMA doesn't know the difference between the real world and Metaverse universes. But for it to be credible, thousands, if not millions, of people will have to take part. We'll also have to create a confrontation so concrete that EMA will have difficulty distinguishing it from reality."

"But that's impossible," said Lidia. "EMA will realize the deception when it sees that the economic indicators aren't changing. A war inevitably leads to economic difficulties: inflation, reduced consumption, massive arms purchases. None of this will change, no matter how realistic your simulation may seem."

"You're right, Lidia," replied Minsky. "In fact, the real solution to our problem lies in degrowth."

"What do you mean by degrowth?" asked Jason.

"It's an important principle based on the realization that the world is finite, with limited resources, and that only a reduction in global production and use can ensure the future of humanity and the preservation of the planet. We need to reduce our consumption, cut back on our lifestyles, restrict our trip, recycle and reuse more. But this change won't happen quickly. It could take years, if not generations. EMA won't have the patience to wait. So, we need to create a diversion."

"By starting a war," said Laurent, thinking of Minsky's idea. "A virtual conflict that won't kill anyone, but that will make EMA believe it has achieved its objective. This will motivate us to make a major shift in our lifestyle."

"Exactly," said Minsky. "I therefore pledge to convince the leaders of all the countries in the EMA network to sign a charter proposing the management of economic degrowth. The results will further confuse EMA, who will see that the fake war will lead to a reduction in our growth."

"But can't EMA interpret international news feeds? If she doesn't see anything, she'll wonder if it's real."

"Of course, and that's why I'm also going to set up a new press agency to spread the word about virtual warfare. Because everyone knows that a conflict can only be won through propaganda. Likewise, all news networks will have to relay false news. I'm ready to finance them to help us."

"Yes, but if some people don't go along with our plan, they'll probably denounce the conspiracy?"

"Maybe, but isn't that the case with all wars? Propaganda works both ways. But it will be confronted with measurable facts about the impact on the economy of our changing habits."

"It's a risky bet," said Laurent. "We have to show the decision-makers in the countries concerned to embark on a 'virtual war.' And the hardest part is getting people to change their behavior."

"I know," said Minsky. "It looks like an uphill battle, and we need to persuade a lot of people. As for the leaders, I'll take care of them. I think I have enough influence in the world to convert them. As for the population, that's your job. You're used to launching propaganda campaigns. I'm sure you'll find a way to get people to change their ways."

"What if we fail?" asked Lidia.

"In fact, we have two choices: either we let EMA's plan succeed and war and suffering decimate humanity, or we try to change things in a sustainable way and adapt our lifestyles and comforts to exist in harmony with nature. I'd rather go for the second option, don't you think?"

Lidia, Jason and Laurent remained silent and meditative for long seconds. They'd never imagined it would come to this. Yes, this plan would lead to major changes in their standard of living and that of billions of people around the world. But they were well aware that this level was artificial. It was only sustained by the massive use of technology. Without it, environmental deterioration would have been much more rapid, and humans would have fallen into a cycle of war and misery. But this technological crutch couldn't last. EMA was a perfect illustration of that. They had to try to change their habits, even if it meant lowering their standard of living. They must focus on degrowth. They must respect the complex system that was the Earth.

"I'm not convinced that people will buy into this idea," said Jason. "It's a lot of sacrifices for some of them."

"I'll grant you that. But I firmly believe that if we're to have any hope of reversing global warming, we must reduce global production and consumption of all goods. Green growth doesn't work. It takes degrowth. What I want to propose to the leaders of our societies is to agree to a new common charter. One that will restore the balance we have deliberately broken.

"Make no mistake," continued Minsky, "degrowth shouldn't be confused with a recession or even a return to the Stone Age. Rather, it's defined as the intentional limitation and reduction of the economy to make it compatible with our planet's biophysical ceilings. In other words, the concept proposes to produce less, share more and decide together. Degrowth thus challenges the dominant paradigm of economic growth at all costs that still prevails in our societies."

Laurent and Jason looked at each other skeptically. They had been beaten and humiliated by Minsky. He understood their doubts.

"I know I've let you down on this adventure. But trust me for the future. I believe I can use my influence and that of EMA to convince the world's leaders. A few years ago, this kind of talk might have been relegated to the margins and considered utopian. But today, with the specter of international conflict and economic collapse looming, the idea of exploring solutions based on the principles of a less frantic, fairer life that isn't measured by the gross domestic product alone will suddenly not seem so extreme to them."

They all looked at each other and realized that reason and common sense meant that they had no choice but to trust Minsky again. They doubted he could succeed, but did they have a choice?

Chapter 27

Minsky, Laurent, Jason and Lidia met again, a few months after the events, at the "Earth Summit" held this year in New York, at the United Nations headquarters.

Held every ten years since 1972, and every year since 2030, the summit brought together world leaders to discuss measures for boosting sustainable development on a global scale.

The assembly had invited Minsky to deliver a speech to its members.

Before going on stage, Minsky met Laurent, Lidia and Jason backstage to check up on them.

"My friends, good to see you again."

He squeezed their hands vigorously, although their confidence in Minsky's sincerity wasn't yet fully established.

"Bonjour, Monsieur Minsky," said Laurent.

"Call me Damien if you don't mind."

"We wanted to talk to you before your speech, so that we could take stock of the situation."

"Go ahead, I'm listening."

"We've thought long and hard about what you said last time about degrowth. And if you succeed in influencing key executives to adhere to your plan, we'll support you in your endeavors. We can't stand in the way of virtue. But we do believe that, if we're to bring this project to fruition, we need to involve EMA in the process, because only she has the necessary neutrality to bring this degrowth to fruition. Submitting this plan to everyone's interests, including yours, Mr. Minsky, is doomed to failure."

"On this point, Laurent, I agree with you," Minsky said. "But we can discuss it later if you like. Foremost, we need to demonstrate to the people in this room the validity of our plan. Now, wish me luck."

"Good luck," smiled Lidia.

Minsky made his entrance, greeted by respectful applause from the assembled crowd. Representatives of various countries and industrial groups were present, all attentive to his words. He made his way to the central podium and discreetly adjusted the miniature microphone concealed in his right ear. A holographic screen projected images of the stage for the audience at the back of the room.

He coughed a little to clear his throat, before starting. The audience fell silent.

"Good evening, ladies and gentlemen. Almost a century ago, in 1988, the Intergovernmental Panel on Climate Change (IPCC) was created by the United Nations and others. This organization was born of an initiative by researchers aware that they were confronted with a problem that was difficult and important to publicize. Since its inception, the IPCC has published numerous reports, sounding the alarm about the climate crisis. At the start of this era, the vast majority of the scientific community implored the authorities and the public to take urgent action. But the personal and electoral ambitions of most governments ignored these warnings.

"At the beginning of the 21e century, well-meaning people like the legendary Bill Gates proposed technological solutions to these problems. Carbon capture, the transition to clean energy and even the reuse of nuclear power were all proposed as remedies that could, a priori, reduce our dependence on fossil fuels. These apostles of technology were betting that we could rely on them while maintaining our high standard of living, and even raising that of less affluent countries."

Minsky pauses before declaring, "But they were wrong!"

"Don't misunderstand me, I've long been a supporter of this technocratic dogma. When I created EMA, I thought I was responding to the environmental consequences of a free market economy. EMA has enabled us to achieve a balance between supply and demand, avoiding waste and reducing overproduction. It has put an end to speculation, which necessarily leads to an imbalance in trade. EMA created green growth on a global scale. All was well until EMA turned against us."

There were murmurs in the room. The audience hadn't expected to hear such a revelation. After waiting for the crowd to calm down, Minsky continued.

"As you know, EMA is the most complex AI ever conceived. It often makes decisions about our economy on its own, because we can't be that efficient. Before intervening in our economy, it runs thousands of simulations to find the best course of action. She looks for the solution that both respects our environment and ensure moderate economic growth. A highly complex, multifactorial problem that only technology can hope to solve.

"But EMA's numerous simulations concluded that the only way to save the planet was ... to eliminate the human race!"

The murmur of the crowd turned into an audible hubbub. People seemed to hear what Minsky wanted to say, but without understanding its implications. Minsky looked at the audience. Jason imagined Minsky's heart was probably racing, and that Minsky himself was anticipating everyone's judgment. He continued.

"EMA had hatched a Machiavellian plan to generate another global conflict aimed at killing each other. It was EMA that triggered the industrial sabotage of recent months. She muddied the waters so that countries would accuse each other. She wanted to provoke a war that would have major consequences for our shrinking populations and falling standards of living. She saw this war as the only way to save the environment and, in a way, humanity in the long term."

The crowd, increasingly indignant, began to grow restless. Some leaders stood up and threatened to leave the room. Minsky, clearly realizing the rising tension, raised his hand to implore them to stay and listen to the end of his story.

"Listen ... listen," Minsky repeated several times in an attempt to calm people down. "Just let me explain."

The crowd died down a little, and Minsky was able to continue.

"It's true that if we analyze his solution purely mathematically, it's exact. The size of the world's population is growing excessively."

People began to get impatient again.

"But ... but," continued Minsky, "fortunately, there's another way that EMA hasn't considered. It's a solution that will require a great deal of courage and sacrifice. The answer, and it's the only one, is to respect our environment and try to pull ourselves out of the ecological doldrums. The answer is economic degrowth."

Minsky waited a few seconds for the audience to fall silent before continuing.

"Everyone knows that human activity has a certain impact on the Earth's ecosystem, just as certain animals and insects do. For as long as humanity has existed, this impact has always been balanced by the ecosystem. But since the 19th century, at the start of the industrial era, we have begun to upset this balance. Our new way of life has led to an increase in population and consumption. We've reached a point where nature is unable to counter our activities fast enough. In systemic terms, we have resonated with nature's imbalance. This has led to abrupt changes in our terrestrial ecosystem. The problem is that, although we're trying to reduce these changes through technology, we aren't succeeding, as we continue to put pressure on the exploitation of the planet's limited resources."

The people in the room were now paying close attention to Minsky's speech.

"From now on, the peoples of the world must reduce their consumption, even if this is to the detriment of their comfort. We must reduce the pressure on resource exploitation and cut back on our use of energy. We need to reuse and recycle more and avoid the superfluous. In short, we need to promote a simpler society based on values of respect for nature rather than greed. This is the only way to achieve a new planetary equilibrium in the long term. A different balance, but a viable balance above all."

One person stood up in the room and shouted: "Yes, but it will take years! It's unrealistic. And how are we going to control EMA?"

"You're right, sir," replied Minsky. "It won't happen overnight. This change in mentality will take years, if not generations. But we have no choice but to achieve it. The alternative is the extinction of the human species."

Minsky continued.

"As for EMA, our team and collaborators around the world have begun to put measures in place to stall her. We've created a Metaverse in which we'll unleash the war EMA so desperately wants. A decoy to make her think her plan is working. In this way, we hope that she will stop her attacks and continue to look after her economy.

"But at the same time, we need to act quickly, because this smokescreen will dissipate in a few years' time. Sooner or later, EMA will see through this deception and resume its attacks. I therefore ask you, at this very moment, to do everything in your power to convince your fellow citizens to lead a more sober life in harmony with nature. A life free of luxury and excess. A new philosophy of life based on voluntary simplicity and respect for nature.

"So, I propose—no, I beg you—that you sign up to a new charter. The charter of degrowth. This charter will promulgate new values that respect our environment. It will enable us to move towards a society free of individualism, founded on an ideal of cooperation and tolerance. It will advocate a measured use of resources and wealth. It will direct our technological development towards mitigating its impact on the quality of life of our citizens, rather than towards increasing wealth. It will offer us the chance to accelerate our transition to a more harmonious way of life, respectful of our planet, the cradle of humanity, the mother of us all."

Minsky had finished his speech. A brief silence fell over the hall. After a few seconds, applause was heard, followed by a few more. Like a wave breaking over the room, the applause grew in intensity, spreading throughout the assembly. A feeling of recognition and approval spread through the assembly, saluting Minsky's bold ideas and proposals.

Minsky had won. At least the first round. For the hardest part was yet to come. Educate the people of Earth to reduce their lifestyle. This was essential for the survival of the species.

Chapter 28

A few weeks after Minsky's historic speech at the Earth Summit, Lidia, Laurent and Jason found themselves invited to California by Minsky, now convinced of his candor and certain that he wasn't imagining a double game. The Möbius team had helped Minsky's team set up the virtual war as a diversion for EMA.

Minsky welcomed his three new friends with open arms. Laurent shook Minsky's hand, this time more warmly. He no longer doubted Minsky's sincerity or his ability to execute his plan.

"First, we wanted to thank you for getting the Total War Metaverse up so quickly. It's very realistic. We've managed to persuade millions of gamers to take part. It's a huge success. It allows some people to vent their excess aggressivity. We've also integrated several intelligent agents to ensure a constant presence of troops in the Metaverse. Hostilities can now officially begin."

"But the biggest thing remains to be done," said Jason. "Convincing eleven billion human beings to change their mentality and adhere to the principles of the charter. That means a lot of sacrifices for some."

"I share your concern," replied Minsky. "That's why my team has developed a unique experience that everyone in the Metaverse can try out, and which will eventually change their minds. An experience so enriching that they'll have no choice but to subscribe to my plan."

"What's it all about?" asked Lidia.

"It's hard to describe. In fact, it would be better if you experienced it for yourselves. So, I'd like to take you all on a little journey into EMA's consciousness to understand all the issues she deals with on a daily basis. It'll convince you, I'm sure. Are you willing to give it a try?"

With nothing to lose, they decided to accept.

"That's the spirit," said Minsky. "You'll see; you won't regret it."

Minsky asked Lidia, Jason and Laurent to follow him into the Metahub room. He invited them to sit down.

"What you're about to experience," explained Minsky, "is an unparalleled immersive experience. An experience that will change your perception of the world. And your perception of EMA."

"Yes, but what makes your application different from all the others already in the Metaverse," asked Lidia?

"Excellent question," replied Minsky. "Our experts have developed a way of conditioning people prior to their experience in the Metaverse. They'll be conditioned before the session to open their minds. This produces the same effect as a psychotic drug, making your brain more receptive to external suggestions.

"Isn't it dangerous," asked Jason?

"It's perfectly safe, and quite pleasant, too. You'll feel a certain euphoria."

The three friends settled into their seats. Jason's Metahub crown descended quietly towards his head. Everything around him went black.

As soon as he was transported into the Metaverse, he heard a soft, soothing voice suggesting that he was calm down and relax. Jason was beginning to see the effects of hypnosis. Everything around him became brighter. His senses became sharper, more attuned to his surroundings. It was as if he'd been given superpowers. He was calm and serene, and temporarily closed his eyes.

When he opened them again, he found himself in a lush garden filled with flowers and plants of every color. He could hear the sounds of nature, like birds singing and water slowly flowing in a stream not far from him. He immediately felt at peace and in harmony with his surroundings. The warm rays of the sun gently caressed his skin. A delicate fragrance of lavender perfume wafted through the air. Birds chirped and fluttered effortlessly between the branches. Jason marveled at what he was observing. He felt as if he'd been transported to another world, a world of peace and infinite possibilities.

He had a feeling he'd been here before, even if he couldn't really remember. It felt like paradise. "This is it!" he exclaimed. "This is paradise. The origin of humankind. He felt it. He understood it."

Suddenly, everything around him changed. He was absorbed into a virtual vortex that projected him into another world. Everything around him was moving very fast. Warriors were fighting barbaric enemies with swords. He saw men and women burned alive at the stake. He saw conquistadors kill and slaughter hundreds of natives. He saw Black slaves whipped to blood by white masters. He saw bombs fall on soldiers in wet trenches. He saw all kinds of horrific events rushing past him. He saw the dark side of human history accelerated. He understood that all these events were the result of the human ego and the thirst for power and domination. He understood this.

The scenes changed again. He saw men, pulling huge stones, building a pyramid. He saw masons laying a keystone for a cathedral. He saw ships crossing the sea to a New World. He saw a scientist look through the lens of a microscope for the first time. He saw a man cranking an old car. He saw a woman in front of a computer screen scrolling through millions of numbers. He saw a rocket take off with a crew and launched to Mars. He saw a humanoid robot helping elderly people to get out of bed. He witnessed humankind's genius. He understood it.

He was swept into another vortex. There he saw huge factory chimneys belching plumes of black smoke. He saw tons of sewage flowing directly into a river. He saw fires out of control, making the atmosphere unbreathable. He saw mountains of plastic garbage flown over by a few seagulls. He saw huge traffic jams in an overcrowded city. He saw the consequences of human activity. He understood it.

He was swept away again. He saw people coming together to clearly defend the environment. He saw groups of people planting trees to replace those that had been cut down. He saw scientists working to find ecological alternatives to current production methods. He saw schools and universities teaching their students about the importance of nature conservation and sustainable development. He saw humankind's efforts to right his wrongs and protect the planet. He understood all that.

The scenes changed once again. He saw children playing in parks and on beaches. He watched families laughing and having fun together. He saw friends having a drink and discussing their lives. He saw lovers strolling hand in hand through flower gardens. He saw elderly people watching the sunset in peace. He saw all the beautiful things of life had to offer. He saw the beauty of life. He understood it.

He was finally thrown into a final whirlwind, back to the place where it all began, the original Eden. He wished it could last forever, it felt so good.

Jason was deeply moved by what he had just experienced. He felt as if he'd seen the history of humankind in accelerated form, from the birth of man to the present day. He had seen humankind's moments of glory and genius, but also its darker moments and its damaging consequences for the environment. It was undeniable that this experience had opened his eyes to the reality of humanity's place in the universe.

Suddenly, his peripheral vision narrowed more and more. He saw a light intensify to the point of blinding him. He woke up in his seat, convinced he'd had a unique experience. Suddenly, he sat up and shouted, "I now understand!"

Epilogue

Jason stood carefully tending his garden. He relished the physical labor and the contact with nature. With his hands covered with soil, he felt connected to the earth that nourished his plants. Since the end of his adventure, he now shared his daily life with Lidia, his new partner. They had decided to lead a simpler life in harmony with nature, growing their own food on their small farm. It was a choice that filled them with happiness and satisfaction, far from the hustle and bustle of the technological world.

Since the EMA event, Minsky had rewarded him with this small plot of land. He thanked him for his contribution to EMA's new project. With his invention of molecular traceability, he had been able to make EMA's interventions in the global economy more precise.

Lidia called out to him at the end of the row. She beckoned him to come to the house, as he was receiving a visitor. Jason hurried to join Lidia and wondered who it was.

He arrived at the house and took off his boots before entering the kitchen. He saw Minsky, sitting quietly with a cup of tea in his hand.

"Jason!" said Minsky. "Good to see you again. How's life as a farmer?" he quipped.

"I'm very pleased. But I never thought it would be this hard. There's always something to do. I don't have time to get bored."

"Great! Lidia tells me you've bought some goats?"

"Yes, to milk them and make good cheese. But you didn't come here to talk about my goats, I imagine."

"No, no. I was in the neighborhood and thought I'd give you an update on EMA, and our plan. As you're the instigators of this reform, if I can call it that, I wanted to keep you up to date."

"Good idea," said Lidia. "With the work on the farm, we don't get out much and sometimes forget to listen to the news. What's happened since you spoke to the leaders?"

"The good news is that the majority of governments have ratified the international charter that will ensure an economy based on degrowth. This will have an impact on our consumption and production capacities in our economy."

"That won't sit well with many politicians," remarked Jason.

"That's right. This charter sounds the death knell of a society where politicians win elections by promising ever more growth, and analysts applaud the slightest increase in consumption."

"And the bad news?" asked Lidia. "Because where there's good news, there's always bad news, isn't it?"

"You're right," laughed Minsky. "Well, the problem is the war. In fact, I should say the 'virtual war' we've started to distract EMA. In order to achieve a true degrowth economy, this will take years and even generations. This will force us to maintain a virtual conflict for longer than expected. So long that it makes no sense, even for an artificial intelligence. We have to stop this conflict sooner or later; otherwise EMA will realize the deception. The current economy doesn't adequately reflect a real war."

"But how are you going to control EMA?" asked Lidia.

"Well, I've managed to influence governments to stop this war and ask EMA to manage the degrowth treaty, signed by the major countries. EMA will therefore be responsible for reducing demand by intervening directly in cryptonomics, to ensure a gradual and peaceful slowdown of the economy. As a result, other countries such as China have shown an openness to joining the EMA's economy. Cryptonomics is poised to become the largest integrated economy in human history. EMA inherits the enormous role of ensuring that our's shrinks while limiting inconvenience to the population, but also respecting the limited capacity of the planet's resources."

"The next few years are going to be difficult," commented Lidia. "Everyone has to find their share of happiness, just like EMA. Jason and I now own this little piece of paradise. Thanks to you. We're very grateful."

"I'm glad to hear it. And I'm happy for you."

"What are your plans for finding your happiness?" asked Jason of Minsky.

"For me, it's simple. My only desire is to take care of EMA. Although we can't rely on technology alone to save us, EMA will enable us to better control our economy and prevent the drifts that will inevitably occur."

With these words, full of wisdom, the three accomplices knew that the game wasn't up. The future of humankind lay not in their hands, but in the actions of each and every one of Earth's citizens.

The planet had always respected mankind by nourishing and protecting him. It is high time they did the same.

Don't miss out!

Visit the website below and you can sign up to receive emails whenever Aian D. Grey publishes a new book. There's no charge and no obligation.

https://books2read.com/r/B-A-ZCBAB-UKKNC

BOOKS 2 READ

Connecting independent readers to independent writers.

Did you love *EMA*? Then you should read *Why ChatGPT is a Game-Changer*[1] by Denis Boulanger Ph.D.!

[2]

In November 2022, OpenAI launched ChatGPT, a groundbreaking natural language processing technology that uses deep learning algorithms to generate and create new text content, signaling a potential shift in how we interact with computers.

Despite its immense popularity, this new technology has raised questions about its potential threat to content creators. Should we embrace this revolutionary tool, or be concerned about its impact?

1. https://books2read.com/u/mdXWVd
2. https://books2read.com/u/mdXWVd

This book is for all technophiles who are fascinated by the advances of artificial intelligence but wonder in which direction this technology is heading. Should we perceive AI as a menace or a collaborator that will elevate our intelligence to unprecedented levels?

.

Read more at denisboulanger.ca/index.html?lang=en.

Milton Keynes UK
Ingram Content Group UK Ltd.
UKHW021535101023
430299UK00014B/560